Travis I. Sivart

# The Once & Future Jack

# The Traveller's Inn, Book 4

Travis I. Sivart

Travis I. Sivart

The Once & Future Jack

The Traveller's Inn, Book 4

Copyright © 2025 Travis I. Sivart

**Talk of the Tavern Publishing Group**

Travis I. Sivart

## Dedication

For Jamie, Ed, Maria, and Steve. Altogether, you're JEMS.

Travis I. Sivart

# Table of Contents

Travis I. Sivart

## 1. Into the Void

Jack sat in the dark, elbows on knees and chin resting heavily on his palms. He drew in a deep, slow breath, held it for a few seconds, then let it wind out from his chest like a tea kettle slowly morphing into a whoopee cushion. He wasn't sure what this place was, where it was, or how he got here, but he thought it probably wasn't the basement of the Traveller's Inn.

The Traveller's Inn was his baby and his home. It was like living inside of a time-travelling, dimension-hopping whale, if cetaceans were made of wood and stucco or neon and steel. Oh, that was another thing, the building could change its appearance. The same way someone might change their clothes when they went out, selecting the style based on the place they were going. Well, the inn could do that also, inside and out. Jack had seen it as a futuristic dance club, an old west saloon, a medieval pub, a desert tent made of woven goat hair, a corner hole-in-the-wall dive bar, and even a submarine.

Travelling to feudal Japan was as simple as heading on a weekend trip for Jack. He'd taken the building to places that were home to dragons, apocalyptic gangsters, regular gangsters, zombies, ogres, kings, cyborgs, and that was the short list. The place always had various and sundry rooms that would be appropriate for the time and place it travelled, but it hadn't had a basement in a long time. Jack wasn't sure why it hadn't had one. Or maybe it did, but it didn't show it to him or the others. The inn could be like that sometimes. It was like it had a mind of its own.

He'd come down to the basement looking for Wanderly. The small man was capable, but curious and chaotic in nature. It wasn't out of character for him to wander off—as befit his name—and get into various types of trouble. Jack expected that, but still went looking for him because of odd circumstances involving the inn. It wasn't like Wanderly snuck off to commit his usual minor mischief, he'd gotten lost in the inn. And that was unusual because the halfling had once run the place and had known it inside and out.

But Jack had gone down the stairs to search for his friend ages ago. Hours? Years? Longer? He couldn't be sure. Time can be that way when it has little meaning and space is just a canvas you paint a picture on. And Jack was a painter. He created realities with little effort and had enough time to do so. Because when you lived inside and outside of time and space, nothing was very difficult when it came to the manipulation of time and space.

Living on borrowed time was when it became hard to create. But he didn't live on time—or a timeline—not like normal people did. But he could visit them. He could pop in, hang out a shingle, and do his business until it was time to move on to the next place. But in this case, this particular time, everything felt borrowed. It was like Jack wasn't in control of his travelling ability.

Wrinkling his brow, Jack wondered if he created the next place or was it someone else's place and he just visited. If it was just a visit, then he brought his own furniture for the duration of his stay and made himself at home. It was only right, because he was here to help and with that came a certain amount of creative freedom.

"That's not right," Jack mumbled, his voice thick with disuse. "I don't get carte blanche for just showing up."

"But maybe you should, wouldn't you agree?" asked a familiar, echoing baritone. "If you arrive to assist in the making of a better future, why wouldn't you be entitled to certain creature comforts and allowances for what you do?"

Jack felt he should know the voice. It was as familiar as the tickle on the back of his neck after a haircut. Some loose bit of hair that wasn't quite attached but still lingered. Or was it a wee bit that the barber missed?

Shifting his eyes to look for the voice, Jack realized he was no longer in the dark. Well, not completely in the dark. He was sitting on something but couldn't tell what. Raising his head, he looked for the source of the voice and anything else. He could see himself, but the area around him appeared to be an endless deep grey flat plain. Not grass or sand, but a simple surface that expanded away from him. There wasn't even a horizon. And he wasn't in a spotlight. In fact, there wasn't a source for the light.

"If I'm entitled to certain comforts," Jack said to no one in particular, because there wasn't anyone particularly there, "then I think I'm on a lawn chair. And there's a bit of water in front of me, so I can watch the ripples and movement."

The things he mentioned were there, like they'd always been there, and he'd just noticed them. The lawn chair was one of the old ones with an aluminum frame and plastic fiber straps interwoven to make the seat and back. In front of him was a stone wall, not quite knee height. In curved in a circle away from him, creating a well that was about twice his height across. The surface rippled, small rings of movement bumping into one another and lightly lapping against the low wall.

"Not quite what I had in mind." Jack wiggled in the creaky chair and found it was now a maroon nylon camp chair with a cup holder in the right arm. "That's a little better."

"Jack," the disembodied voice chided, "I thought you'd be better at this. You have the ability to make whatever you want, and you landed on a cheap chair and a primitive well?"

"It's comfortable and good enough for my needs at the moment," Jack said, sounding a little defensive and embarrassed.

"And that's why you're here, isn't it? Because you're satisfied with 'good enough' and being 'comfortable' is why the Traveller's Inn showed you the basement."

The voice fell quiet, leaving the words hanging without explanation. Jack sat back in the camping chair, scooching his butt up a little and dropping his arms onto the rests at his side. He wriggled again, shifting to one side, then the other. Settling down, he stared at the ripples in the contained pool in front of him. There seemed to be two main sources of the disturbances, and a half dozen smaller ones. They all overlapped and rolled around and across one another, but the two main ones always dominated the well, one slightly stronger than the other.

Leaning forward, Jack studied the eddies closer and swore he could see something below each. Squinting and scooting forward in his chair, the back legs came off the ground and Jack nearly toppled into the well. Flailing his arms and throwing himself back, Jack fell and landed on the ground which was now hard-packed earth, and a small cloud of dirt rose around him.

"Did you shove me?" Jack asked, looking around for the chair that had been there a moment ago.

"Jack," the voice sighed, "someone has to do it. Either you fight to survive, or you fall and disappear into the waters. That's what good enough and comfortable gets you. Nothing. But it allows others to do what they want since you're not doing anything to move forward."

"And that's what you're doing?" Jack accused with a sneer. "You're doing what you want to do because I'm not doing enough for you?"

"This isn't about me, Jack," the voice sighed, "this is about you. About what you do. And inaction is still doing something. It's getting out of the way so others may do things. You made a choice when you sent everyone else scurrying to do things but avoided doing anything yourself."

Jack flinched as if he'd been hit, then looked around. He wasn't sure if he was checking to see if the source of the voice saw him flinch, or if he was looking for something to lash back at. This had been a discussion that had come up more than once recently.

"You're him, aren't you?" Jack looked up at the empty sky

and saw there was a sky now.

A dim glow of distant stars and a half dozen planets were fading into view. It was like he'd been in bright light (though it had been quite the opposite) and his eyes were adjusting to the dark. A red orb about the size of a grapefruit hung in the sky near a horizon that hadn't been there a moment before. A few hand spans to one side was an immense purple and blue planet with glittering rings and a rainbow hue moving around them until it disappeared behind it. A silvery sphere partially covered an orange and yellow circle behind it, and a green and gold planetoid in the distance moved in a fast orbit around a brown husk of a planet with huge, blackened craters.

Comets whipped across the firmament in twos and threes. Or maybe they were asteroids or meteors, but they had scintillating tails trailing them, and Jack seemed to recall that asteroids were different, and meteors were asteroids entering the atmosphere. As the information came into his head, a score of rocks hit the visible dome of the small planet he was on and light up brilliantly as they scattered into the distance, slight tremors evidence of their ground fall.

"Where am I?" Jack whispered to himself. "This isn't Earth or Aetheria…"

"Sorry, Jack," came the disembodied voice, "that's for me to know and you to find out. But I will tell you this; you've always limited yourself. You have this incredible power over so many things, but you've done so little with it. Isn't it time that you did more? Or let someone else take charge for a while and shake things up?"

"Shake things up?" Jack asked, pushing to his feet. He looked up, then around him. "You know it's annoying to keep talking to myself? Can't you come out where I can see you?"

"No, Jack, I cannot. Not until you decide you can see me, and you haven't done that."

"Who *are* you?" Jack asked.

"That's the question, isn't it?" the voice asked. "Who could I be? I know a lot about you, and I can show you things that made you who you are. Let's play a game, shall we?"

"I don't like playing games," Jack spat.

"But you do though, don't you?" the disembodied voice sounded like it was smiling. "That's all you do, play games. And you play games with other people's lives. The regulars of the inn, the people you drew to Aetheria when they were dying on Earth, and all your interactions once you left your original timeline. It was all games, and frankly, you haven't gotten any better at them since you started. Shouldn't you have been learning, growing, and leveling up—to use an appropriate term?"

"Those weren't games." Jack shot back. "I was helping people or finding the right people to help others."

"Were you, Jack?" the voice chided. "I mean, were you really helping others and not playing games? We can take a look. Let's call the well you created the Well of Knowledge. It's a font of experience and wisdom, a source of hindsight. We can use it to confirm if you're right, or if I'm right."

"Speaking of right," Jack took an involuntary step toward the well, "what gives you the right to do this? Who gave you the power to do this to me, to everyone involved? What happened to the others who entered the basement? Are you toying with them like you're toying with me?"

"Jack," the answer was a throaty laugh, "you're the one who has been toying with them and with me. Lurking at the edges of something so much larger, pulling the puppet strings, and sending others into dangerous situations because you were too much of a coward to take the plunge yourself."

Jack found himself on the edge of the well, his toes scraping the edge of the low wall that didn't come up to his knees. The celestial bodies above were distorted images in the water resembling a Salvador Dali painting. What were round planets looked like melting disks of color. The ripples showed forms below them, reaching for the reflections and trailing fingers through them.

"Wait," Jack said, stumbling backwards.

His legs hit something, and he fell onto a plush recliner. Looking at the armchair, it looked like a throne blended with a La-Z-Boy chair, if it was made for a giant, or if he was a small child.

"Comfortable, Jack?" the voice asked. "Is it easier to sit down, lean back, and let others change the world rather than to do it yourself? Or are you a coward? Afraid to take charge and do things yourself?"

"No," Jack said quietly, then with more authority, "no. I know I can't do it. If I take a direct hand in events, it only comes to destruction and chaos. I've avoided it for a long time, and I don't plan to do that if I can avoid it."

"Forest fires make way for fresh growth, Jack," the voice said, like it was explaining something obvious to a school kid. "Floods that wash away the top layer of the land allows new crops to grow. You can't make an omelet without breaking a few eggs. This is the way nature intended things to be. We learn through our mistakes. How will you ever grow if you won't risk anything?"

"You don't win a chess game by making mistakes," Jack countered. "It's through watching the game, careful planning and knowing how your opponent plays, that you win."

"But life isn't as black and white as a chessboard and pieces, Jack, you know that." The voice smiled again. "Life is messy, and you have to get your hands dirty to do anything. Even building a house leads to blisters and sore muscles, and sometimes you hit your thumb with your own hammer. To plant crops and grow something nourishing, you have to get filthy, and then wash up afterwards. No one will remember that you were a dirty, dirty boy. They only see you afterwards and praise you for the fruits of your labors. A new building, a plentiful harvest, and these things benefit others. Anyone who argues these points just wants to sit and complain about how things change, denying progress and forward movement in life. Are you a whiner, Jack? Are you a complainer, Jack? Or do you want to accomplish great things to benefit everyone that will come after you're gone?"

"You're twisting things," Jack breathed. "I *have* been moving forward."

"Have you, Jack?" The voice took on a dangerous tone. "Let's take a look at what you've done, shall we? Look into the Well of Knowledge and we can explore your claims together."

The water swirled, the smaller ripples becoming sharper though they didn't grow any larger. The colors from above shifted and became a room and showed an old man sitting at a bar.

## 2. Drunken Master

Croaker Norge, detective and gadgeteer, looked around, then returned his gaze to the glass in front of him. He didn't know what else to do—or even if there was anything else to do—besides sit here and drink. The whiskey was good, though. It didn't really taste yummy or anything, but it tasted comforting. Kitty once asked him what he got out a drink, and he'd replied with an 'ah' sound followed by lip smacking.

It took the edge off things. The drink wasn't the enemy, and it wasn't the answer. It was the cloth-thin material of a tent insulating him from the rest of the world. It also gave him time to process things while he had something to fiddle with, the same for smoking his pipe. He didn't especially enjoy pipe smoking, but it gave him time to think, to organize his thoughts, and people tended to wait when he was messing with these tools. Dysfunctional tools, he knew that, but they were what he had to work with.

Lifting the glass, he swirled the amber liquid. The glass was no longer clear where he could look through it to watch people in the mirror behind the bar. It was rough, cloudy, like they hadn't figured out how to make glasses right yet. But they had. Things were just regressing. He also wasn't on a bar stool and being waited on by Cogsley. The bar wasn't there anymore. It was a couple planks of wood set atop a couple of barrels. That made it too low to lean on. And the barstools were gone.

Cogsley wasn't working the same anymore, either. It was as if the automaton had come down with some weird affliction. Normally the bartender and quasi-manager of the Traveller's Inn stood tall and flicked unseen pieces of lint or dirt from his tux and tails, or from the top hat which normally rested on his lightbulb-like head with white-gloved hands. Now, the machine-man leaned against a post, rubbing his glass dome, and muttering to himself and shaking his head.

Croaker studied the glass again and saw a dozen grains of sand dancing in the liquid whirlwind. He shrugged and threw it back, slurping a little. He'd had worse. But he wasn't sure if he'd seen the Traveller's Inn in worse shape. It was like it was breaking down as well. The people were mostly missing, and the drinks were getting coarser, and the furniture was falling to pieces when he wasn't looking.

He pushed his fedora brim up and out of his eyes, reached into this duster, pulled out his pipe and tobacco pouch, and begin packing a bowl. He did this slowly, while turning to take in the peeling paint and warping wood that was an industrial rave warehouse not too long ago. Hours ago? No, it must have been a few days at least. Maybe a week or two? He couldn't be sure. But canvas walls and thin warped and weathered wood had replaced burnished steel and neon. And more changes were happening every time he looked around.

He'd been figuring things out, solving mysteries, foiling crimes, and facing down things that shouldn't exist all his life. Well, at least since his teens when he left home and went to the port city of New Sileans. But he was old now, and too tired to care about doing all that. Jack was missing, Wanderly was missing, Cogsley was sick, and the dozen or so people who usually frequented the establishment had gone out to explore the surrounding wasteland of scrub bushes and tangled thorns.

There we a few people still here, if you wanted to call them that. There was Cogsley, of course, he never left. Golem was in the corner of the place, standing next to a flapping panel of canvas, leaning on their broom and staring at their counterpart, Cogsley. Was that a look of disgust on the construct's face? Anger? Golem was huge, much larger than before, and towered over everyone at nearly two and a half meters, the thick clay body filling out and shaping into what was beginning to look like corded muscles.

Elementius and Tilbert sat at a makeshift table, their heads together, and whispering like they were planning a heist and didn't want anyone else to hear them. Elementius was a snooty book type, some sort of professor at a university Croaker had never heard of. Tilbert was his underfed and nervous sycophant. The younger man nodded and smiled without any enthusiasm, typing on his magical typewriter. It was more of a court stenographer machine, if those things wrote shorthand in a weird language that Croaker had never seen before, despite having been a dozen worlds, and done investigations in more than a few of them.

Shaking his head and sighing, Croaker shook his head and raised his drink to his lips. The glass was now a ceramic cup, and it was empty, only muddy dregs remaining at the bottom. Staring at the bottom where whiskey should be, Croaker stared at the words swirling where the alcohol normally waited. He scrunched his eyes to slits, looked away, then looked back into the cup.

"Okay," he muttered, "I understand. I don't like it, but I get it. It doesn't tell me much of what I'm supposed to do, but I'll come up with something."

"I'm sorry, sir," Cogsley said, leaning on the pole for support, "what did you say?"

"What?" Croaker looked up, his mind coming into sharp focus. "What did you just say?"

"I asked you what you said, sir," the automaton slurred, his words blurred and slow.

"No," Croaker shook his head, "what were the exact words you just said?"

"I am sorry, sir, what did you say?" Cogsley echoed, a question in the question.

"Nuh uh," Croaker waggled a finger at the machine-man, "you said '*I'm* sorry'. You used a contraction."

"Oh, come on," came the crisp, proper sound of

Elementius's voice. "leave him alone. Can't you see he's in distress? Don't harangue the man for using less formal language in his obvious moment of distress."

Croaker turned his head and shoulders toward the professor and squinted. Tilbert was nodding vigorously and pointing at Elementius as if to say, "yeah, what he said. That's right, don't you agree?"

"Shut up, Tilbert," Croaker spat, and both men looked surprised at the admonition. "And as for you, Elementius, are you doing anything useful to help figure out what's going on here? Why is the place falling apart? What's going on with Cogsley? And you two are acting as if nothing is happening, sitting there whispering like you were…"

Croaker waved both hands in small circles and the clay cup slipped from his fingers and crashed to the floor, shattering. When he looked down at it, it had turned to wet clumps of brown dirt and melted into the dirt floor that had been concrete not too long ago.

"You're drunk," Elementius said, his face flushed and wrinkled into something Croaker couldn't tell if it was anger or embarrassment. "Raving like a lunatic. Perhaps you should take a walk. You could go find the others."

"You want me to go out there?" Croaker waved at the sand and sawgrass outside, his gaze following his gesture.

Outside of the inn were endless rolling hills covered with mostly low, brown vegetation hanging on to windblown dirt and rock. A thin, muddy trickle that once may have been a stream wound around the stumpy hillocks, and a dull orb of mustard color that was the sun moved slowly around the edge of the horizon, a haze distorting the thick air.

"We're observers," Elementius continued, without responding to the question, "and observing is our job. We are not men of action, nor do we desire to be. Isn't that the way of things? Tilbert, don't you agree? This man is unhinged and distraught, and it would be best if he just left the premises?"

"Oh, yes, Elementius," Tilbert nodded twice in precise movements. "We're scholars. We're studying the events here, not directing them. And your wisdom knows no bounds.

Perhaps it would be better if Mister Norge were to depart. I think he's outlived his usefulness within the inn."

"You want me to remove him, Master Elementius?" a deep rumble asked, and Golem stepped forward to stand behind the two men.

"Who sent you to observe?" Croaker asked quietly, almost to himself.

"What?" Elementius choked, standing up and Tilbert mimicking the action. "What sort of question is that? Are you accusing us of something nefarious? Maybe Golem *should* throw you out."

The hulking form of the construct took a step forward and Croaker held up his hands, dropped his head, and deflated.

"No," he sighed. "No, that won't be necessary. You're right, I overreacted. I'm just a tired old man who got worked up because I'm worried about what happened to Jack. I'll keep quiet and try to remember my place here."

"Hmph," Elementius grunted, then looked around. "It's fine, Golem. Let him stay, unless he has another outburst. We don't have time for that sort of behavior."

Golem grumbled, a sound like gravel shifting underfoot. "I'll return to my duties and see to the maintenance of this building, but I will be ready if you need me."

"That won't be necessary," Croaker smiled weakly. "I'm just going to smoke my pipe, help Cogsley, and maybe get another drink."

The old man hunched to his feet, limped around the makeshift bar, stopped at a lamp to light his pipe with a strip of cedar he drew from his duster. He pulled a bottle of whiskey from the barback, poured a healthy helping into a fresh clay cup—which was now taller and had a handle—and moved towards Cogsley, puffing on his pipe. Elementius and Tilbert sat down and returned to their whispering, shooting furtive glances in the direction of the bar.

Croaker moved to Cogsley's side, juggling his pipe and drink. He stuck the pipe between his teeth and put his free hand on Cogsley's upper arm to get the automaton's attention.

"You doing okay, buddy?" Croaker asked.

"Not in the least, sir," Cogsley replied. "Would you like me to expand on the issues I am currently facing, or did you come to my side for ulterior motives?"

"Well, both to be honest," Croaker gave a tight grin. "I think knowing what you're going through can help with my investigation."

The wire inside Cogsley translucent dome raised a bit, the equivalent of anyone else raising their eyebrows in surprise.

"You're on a job, sir?" the bot asked.

"Call me Croaker, Cogs. I think it's appropriate considering everything that's going on, especially if my suspicions pan out." Croaker gave a little huff, a cross between a sigh, an expression of exasperation, and an ironic laugh. "I think with Jack and Wanderly missing, others might be trying to move in."

"And this is information is safe to share with me?" Cogsley asked. "How do you know I haven't been compromised?"

"You might be soon," Croaker paused to remove the pipe and take a drink, then went on, "but right now, I think you're a victim. You're a creature of Jack's. I'm a creature of Jack's. I think others may be on a different side."

"How do you mean, sir?" Cogsley asked.

"Croaker," the old man corrected without thinking, "and I think that because Jack invited me in. You showed up shortly after he reclaimed control of the inn from Wanderly. But he invited Wanderly. And Nomed. And many of the others. But some folks," Croaker shot a meaningful glance towards the other side of the room, "came in on their own. Or because someone else sent them, including those two and Golem."

"I see," Cogsley's coiled element in his head drew down and together in concentration, "and what is to be done about the situation?"

"I could go down to the basement," Croaker said, "though the door is now a trapdoor in the floor and look for Jack and Wanderly. But I don't think that would help. I think we need to stay up here and keep the place ready for when they return."

"What does that mean?" Cogsley asked, looking around. "What exactly do you need to do, and how can I help? I can barely stand. I think I have a cold, or whatever the equivalent is for me. I am weak, and my thoughts are broken. Muddled is the word that would apply to you. I feel disconnected and everything I perceive seems to be disconnected. This conversation is like serving drinks on a busy night with the music loud and a fog in the room, but it is all silent. I do not think that makes sense, but it is the best I can describe it."

"I just need to know where to start to fix this place," Croaker glanced around, a hopeless look crossing his face. "How do I fix it? I'm good with gadgets, and this place is just a huge gadget but on a level beyond the physical. I don't know. On a psychic level? Magical?"

"Maybe you should consult the owner's manual?" Cogsley suggested.

"The what?" Croaker looked at the automaton, his eyebrows climbing up his forehead. "There's an instruction book?"

"Jack has been keeping notes," Cogsley nodded and drew out a small sheaf of papers, "and entrusted me with its safekeeping. But be warned, it may change or deteriorate as the inn does so as well."

"So," Croaker took the papers and shoved them into his duster, "this may turn to dust, or just be wrong as this place does the same?"

"Indeed," Cogsley's speech slowed, then stuttered, "wh-wh-which is why I think they may be best held by someone else."

"Well," Elementius's voice cut through the quiet conversation, "look at that."

Croaker jerked in surprise, snatching the papers and stuffing them in his overcoat, then looking over his shoulder at the man.

"The intrepid adventurers are returning," Elementius pointed out of the building that was nothing more than a large one room tent now.

Croaker looked where he was pointing and saw a collection of figures converging on the Traveller's Inn. They walked in groups of two mostly and were trudging across the top of a hill in the distance.

"Nomed and Wanderly are the key," Cogsley said quietly. "Darome and Durg are the heart and soul. The other six are new, but they play a part. The wit of Mogits, the cleverness of Manx, the fire in Kitty and Fritz, and Sam and Tiffene to constantly question, fight, and confuse."

"What?" Croaker turned back to the automaton. "Say that again? Who is what? How do you know? Give me something more?"

Cogsley slumped, one hand still gripping the pole and sparks visibly rolling across the element in his head. The light slowed, and the wire became a dull glow like a lightbulb that's about to die.

"Cogsley," Croaker reached out with a free hand and shook the bartender. "Cogsley, I need to know more about everything. Don't leave me here alone. Are they here to help or destroy the inn?"

The automaton didn't answer, and even if he did, Croaker wouldn't have heard it over the shouts from the group approaching the inn.

## 3. Out of Sight

Darome was small, even for a gnome. He rode on the shoulder of his best friend and personal bodyguard, Durg  He met the ogre half-breed when they ran into each other in a prison. Evil wizard, power-hungry warlord, and all that. It's a tale as old as time. But they broke out, overthrew the dictators. and became best buds. But it hadn't been Darome's idea. Durg had approached him with a plan: the big guy would tear the metal bar door off its hinges, keep the guards off the miniature spellslinger, and Darome would do the rest. After all, according to Durg, the gnome would be the brains of the operation.

Darome, always cocky—though rarely overconfident in his own mind—had agreed immediately. What could have been better than someone who strokes his ego and makes sure he doesn't get punched in the face, a sword in the guts, or even worse…punted? People loved punting gnomes. Which is silly, because physics dictated aerodynamics, and gnomes were never streamlined enough to fly right or far. And usually just ended up with broken ribs or a crushed skull from the effort, two things Darome despised despite never having experienced either.

The gnome sat atop the ogre-kin's shoulder and stared at the Traveller's Inn. When he'd last been inside the inn, it had been a weird, huge thing with flashing lights and thumping music with walls. By the time he'd left, it had been a pretty much standard pub from his era, with wood floors and walls and brass and iron fixtures. Now, though, it was a tent. Like the kind that desert people use. The sides were canvas tarps, rolled up to let the wind in. Mind you, it was an enormous tent, but it was still a tent.

Slowing Durg with a slight tug of the ear beside him, the gnome studied the situation. The others streamed towards the tent—pavilion?—without stopping, but Darome needed a moment. Croaker was inside, and the man looked positively upset. Like a racoon who went to wash its food and the morsel melted in the water. He also looked worried, or paranoid. Darome didn't like-like the guy, but he thought Croaker was on the level most days; except when playing cards, then the man was a damned swindler. How dare he out-bluff an illusionist? And he cared about people, even if he claimed most people were idiots. Though if viewed objectively, he wasn't wrong.

The fact that Elementius—the pompous windbag, thinking he knew as much about magic as someone who was out in the field using it—looked as smug as a rat with a wheel of stolen cheese did little for Darome's outlook for what was to come. He'd seen enough in his decades of adventuring to know when something smelled like poo on a shoe.

"What wrong, Darome?" Durg asked what appeared to be a simple question but was actually as layered as the ogre himself. "What you see?"

"It's not what I see," Darome answered, idly rubbing the big guy's earlobe. "It's what I can't see that's bothering me."

"I see," Durg nodded sagely.

"I'm sure you do," Darome chuckled, "but not really. You see, Durg, I'm a master of illusions. It's my passion, my life, and I've been dealing with them for a long time now. I'm used to looking through them and seeing the root of what projected the illusion, its flaws, and the minute beauty that is something that appears so real you overlook it because it is just so common you don't even think twice about it. People often put up illusions, projections of themselves, showing you what they want you to see, rather than what's really there. Do you know what I mean, buddy?"

"Yep, Durg get it," the ogre mix breed nodded again. "People think too much."

"Well, that too, but that's not what I'm getting at. You see Mogits and Manx?" Darome pointed at the two men slogging through the ankle-deep dust covering the ground, and Durg nodded. "They both show a certain side of their personality to you and me and others. Manx shows a surly and moody exterior, but practically begs for people to look inside and see his sensitive side that loves music and poetry. Mogits comes off as the clever trickster, but he's really out to just get some creature comforts without hurting anyone else."

"Yeah," Durg smiled, "they think too much about others. But I got question."

"Yeah, go ahead," Darome patted the big guy's sweaty neck then wiped his hand on his tunic, "how can I help elucidate and educate?"

"When someone nod sagely," Durg asked, "they do it like a smart guy sage, or they seasoning a roast like a cook guy using sage? I like sage in soups. The plant, not the smart guy."

"Aw, you're messing with me because now you think I think too much," Darome giggled and slapped Durg's gigantic gourd of a noggin. "You're a goof, you know that, Durg?"

"Durg know," the half-ogre nodded, "because he taste like sage."

"I don't know what that means," Darome shook his head, "but you're not getting me to lick you again!"

The two grinned and chuckled—one practically a giddy titter, the other giving a gurgling rumble—enjoying the comfortable banter of friends who'd been there for one another, right to the brink of dying or killing.

"I want a point now, Darome," the ogre spawn poked the little guy in the gut with a knobby sausage finger. "Think you smart enough for that?"

"Sure, Durg," Darome let out a small sigh, still smiling and patting his friend, then continued.

Durg listened to his little friend explain about the relationships between the others. The gnome dissected how Kitty and Fritz interacted, how they fought passionately with one another about nothing, and sometimes while laughing, sometimes while growling at one another. Later, they'd always make up, no matter how their fight panned out. Darome pointed out how Sam and Tiffene were constantly angry about something, but Sam from the gut and Tiffene in her head. One reacted loudly volatile, while the other was cold and distant.

Durg thought Darome thought too much, and often thought about what others thought. But knowing how people think was the gnome's job as an illusionist, but he also thought too much about people's thoughts in other ways, too, the way most other people thought. There was a lot of thinking going on, and Durg found it frustrating and exhausting.

The half-ogre had sagely (the wise guy and the good food type, because knowledge was tasty) told Darome he saw, and he knew. The gnome had patted and humored him. But he did see and know. Much more than the gnome. He tried to tell his friend this in simple terms, but the Darome da Gnome had to analyze everything down to the core.

Durg decided it was all too much. It was easier to stand back and watch instead of trying to figure it all out. He had a good friend, a place to live, and people around him who liked him and occasionally needed his help. He liked that. It was the important thing in life, having people, and it made him feel good.

Trailing in behind the ragtag group of his friends, Durg looked around the inn. The place was a mess, a skeleton of what it once was. He could see thin strands of webs connecting the rough-hewn pillars of wood to the flapping canvas covering the space.

Tilting his head, Durg looked at Croaker and Cogsley at the bar. The two were standing close to one another, the metal man leaning on the old man. The professor was watching them, his lips pulled tight and shifting his eyes from Tilbert and back. It smelled like a problem, but in the ogre's head, not his nose. Golem hunched over the mundane tasks he did, but looked like he was upset. That was weird to Durg. The clay man almost never looked mad, just bored or a bit sad.

This was going to be a problem. Durg wasn't worried about the why of things and instead of what was coming. He never planned for a fight, but he knew when someone was looking for one.

As the others settled into whatever places they could find in the room, Darome tugged on his ear, directing him to what was once a bar. The big guy lumbered over, his massive arms swinging, dropped a meaty hand on Croaker's shoulder, and smiled down at the older man.

Mogits began talking, explaining to the room what they found in the barren wasteland outside.

"It's a mess out there," Mogits began with a grand gesture to the sandy dunes, "nothing but tumbleweeds and scrub bushes. The stream is clogged and murky. I mean, we can get water, but we'll want to boil anything before we drink it."

"No animals," Fritz said. "Didn't see a single lizard or bird, didn't smell any either."

"The only interesting thing is a half-buried compass a few hills over," Tiffene added, tugging on her thick, dark braid. "But it was huge. Larger than most buildings. Must be four or five stories tall and that's just the half sticking out of the ground. Looks like it's made of brass, but it wasn't tarnishing like brass."

"Ooh," Sam growled, sweeping his long, red moustache away from his puckered lips. "I hate this place. Like we were sent here to die. Where the tarnation are the others? No sign of footprints and there's not even a light breeze to cover tracks or anything. It's downright creepy."

"They went down into the basement," Manx muttered, brushing his greasy bangs from his eyes. "Don't you remember? Right before things changed."

"Urgh," Kitty pushed her fingers through her short, pink hair. "People, people, don't you get it? There's something going on here. And frankly, I feel like there's nothing we can do. I feel helpless, and that pisses me off."

"Oh, do calm down," Elementius said with a negligent wave of his hand. "There's no need to be reactionary. I think by now we all know that the Inn changes. It changes location and appearance. It's perhaps sometimes challenging to realize the changes for those of a lesser background."

"What's that supposed to mean, Mister Fancy Pants?" Kitty half stood leaning over the barrel she and Fritz shared. "You think you're better than us because you went to some school and got a piece of paper?"

"Well, no," Elementius smirked, "but yes. In this particular area I am better than you. I have studied temporal and interdimensional phenomenon for decades. I've literally written the book on it. People pay me handsome sums for my guidance and advice on such things. Now, if we need some words of wisdom on how to punch someone in the face, or shoot a tin can, then we can look to you."

Kitty had gone red as she leaned over the short barrel and launched herself over it towards the academic. Sam appeared in front of her, grabbing her shoulders and shouting.

"Whoa there, I said whoa there, missy!" he panted, pulling his hands from her and holding them up in front of her. "It's not ladylike to punch an old man, no matter how dad-burned stupid and ignorant he's being, no matter how much of an arrogant ass he's being. It just ain't right. That's the place of a man!"

Sam spun towards the professor, slamming a fist into an open palm and cracking his knuckles. "Prepare yourself for an ass whooping!"

"No," came a rumble from the just behind and to one side of Sam, a thick hand landing on his head and lifting him, "you can't do that."

Sam screamed, his feet kicking out, as Golem turned him in the air to face the automation. Mogits and Manx scooted backwards off their stools, a bright red globe and glinting knives appearing in their hands, respectively. Tiffene stood and held her hands up and frost crackling and coating them up to her elbows, as Kitty drew her vibro-blade and crouched into a low stance.

Durg sighed and rose to his full height, then sucking in a deep breath to belt out a battle shout. He was interrupted by Croaker touching his arm as the old man limped past him and into the center of the room.

"You're all idiots," Croaker barked, snatching the focus of everyone in the room. "I should let you tear each other apart. Kitty put that away. You too, Manx. Mogits, Tiffene, stop doing…" Croaker flapped his hands at them, "whatever you're doing. Golem, put Sam down, gently."

"I would never—" Elementius began, only to be cut off by Croaker spinning to face him.

"Shut your mouth, Professor," Croaker said. "That's your weapon, right? Your words? Your mind? Well, you'll put them away. Use your words to call Golem off. They appear to be your creature now."

The Professor leaned back, color draining from his face and his jaw worked soundlessly. He smacked his mouth closed, then nodded at the automaton. The creature set Sam down, who rubbed at his head and sputtered.

"Go to your corners," Croaker said, sweeping the room with a gaze. "Something is tearing us apart. Maybe it's that Jack is missing, maybe it's something more. But I suggest we all keep our distance from the people we don't get along with before we tear down this building while tearing one another apart. It's a theme, don't you see? Splitting us so we do the work for someone else who is too cowardly to do it themselves?"

Durg nodded sagely as he leaned back down to the planks of the bar, reaching up and patting Darome comfortingly. The gnome took the affectionate pummeling with aplomb, recovering his pointy hat and adjusting it onto his head again.

## 4. Fear Knows No Bounds

"That's the present you created, Jack," the voice chided. "A wonderful duality that's fighting itself. I can show you the past as well. Or the future, but not yours. At least not the future you haven't lived. Of course, here, the future is relative. You took us out of the river of time, and now we only have the stagnant waters of the well to look at. But it's all there, from when you first stepped out of your door into what would become known as ancient Mayan history, or when you triggered the Large Hadron Collider to boost your power through more than time and access the multiverse—to over simplify things—to where you moved so far that the world had changed so much it was a different world."

Jack jerked, hitting his head on the tall wooden back of the chair he sat on. He looked around, checking to see how his seat had changed. It was made of thick, dark wood, and his wrists and ankles were strapped down.

"You restrained me?" Jack asked, his voice cracking.

"No, Jack," the voice was laughing at him again. "You strapped yourself in. Persecution complex much? But I'm as bound as you are until you release us."

"That makes no sense," Jack huffed. "Why would I restrain myself?"

"You said so yourself, to protect others from yourself," the voice replied. "You've reacted to things in the past, but rarely took free action. You're afraid. That fear is holding you back. You're restrained by your own fear. Sound about right?"

"No, it doesn't." Jack pulled on the leather straps.

"Sure, it is," came the answer. "You're a nice guy, Jack. You want people to like you. But it comes off as weak. You may be liked, but you don't command respect if you're always nice, trying to do the right thing to make people happy. To make genuine progress, you gotta piss some people off. That's your measure of how you're doing.

"It's all about fear with you, though, isn't it?" the voice continued. "You're afraid to bother people to get help. You're afraid to upset people by telling them something they don't want to hear, like they're wrong or stupid. Sometimes—a lot of times—you gotta put on your big-boy pants and do what needs done."

Studying his wrists for a moment, Jack then looked out across the endless plain, trying to decide which way would lead to an escape.

"You're living a fucking story book existence, Jack," the voice said, its tone sneering, "a delusional fairy tale. Life rarely has a happy ending, and if it does, then it's temporary. You have to keep working because if your story ends, then you're dead. Is that what you want? I don't think it is, Jack. If I'm right, then you must fight, keep struggling, constantly. Your break is over. Let's get this show on the road, buddy. You need to make the journey, follow the road or turn away from it, and find out what's at the end. I'll even set up three god-damned trials for you of that what you need. Freedom awaits, but only when you choose to take it and not a moment before."

"Like this?" Jack said, holding up his freed wrists, then leaping to the ground between the chair and the well.

As he bolted across the sparse and bleak landscape, a frantic bark of laughter tumbling from his throat, Jack never noticed the two men watching him go.

Nomed crouched behind a flimsy cardboard prop of a scrub bush, looking at it as much as the man fleeing the old-fashioned electric torture chair in front of a well. He looked over at his small companion, Wanderly.

"Why are we here?" he asked, mostly to himself. "I just want to burn the place down. This is all bullshit. Who is he arguing with?"

"Himself?" answered Wanderly to the rhetorical question. "Maybe a higher power? I can't argue with this being bullshit, though. I'd definitely be more poetic about the phrasing. You're so, I don't know. Not dramatic, you've got too much subterfuge built into you for that."

The little man prattled on, as he was prone to do, as Nomed's mind wandered. Wanderly wasn't wrong, Nomed was a man of layers. He was born of a human and aeifain mother and a demon father. He was raised by an aeifain surrogate father who was a wizard who turned to the gods for more power. All his life, Nomed danced back and forth along the lines of what others would call dark and light, right and wrong, chaos and the straight and narrow. Often, he was driven by the urge to upset the status quo. And right now, he really wanted to shake things up, as in set something on fire.

Jack had been an ally, even a friend, for a long time. But Nomed felt stunted by the attention, like Jack was trying to leash him. But also, Nomed wasn't an idiot. He knew Jack wanted to help the greater good, but his methods grated on Nomed.

"Why does this bother me so much?" he muttered.

"Because you're a free spirit," Wanderly answered without hesitation. "I think that's why we get along so well; we both love freedom. Whether that's in choice, or the randomness of the weather. I do love the weather, you know? People like to bitch about the weather being so random, but I always want to point out the beauty of it. I love how it can be blistering hot one day, raining the next, and then frigid in the night."

The little guy wasn't wrong, but he did what he did for fun. At least, that's how it felt to Nomed. Nomed did what he did in logical, surgical methods. He preferred to pick and choose and home in to cut very specific events or plots. Wanderly was all over the place, and in Nomed's view, created chaos randomly.

"But I agree with your question," Wanderly was saying, "and want to know why we're here as well. I mean, I came down to the basement because it felt like the right thing to do. Then you and Jack came down, and you found me, but lost Jack. Then we find him here. Are we here to help him? Or is he here to help us? I think he's gone a little crazy, but hey, that's okay. I think he could use a little crazy. It'll help him if he lets loose a little. He's wound pretty tight most of the time, though he plays it off as being in control. I think he needs to let go and go with the flow, you know?"

"Yeah," Nomed nodded, "and the world has changed again."

"Oh my," Wanderly paused and looked around. "The well and chair are gone. And isn't that the Inn floating above us?"

The landscape changed from a flat, dismal plain to mountainous terrain, sharp ridges of folded land laced with icy trails of snow in the creases, and a broken plateau floating above, fiery wisps of clouds flaring out behind it. A crumbling aged structure surrounding my immense, tarnished cogs sat on the floating island. The gears turned slowly, causing the building to shift and shed stones during the tremors. A field of rolling clouds shifted in the distance behind, tumbling like an angry ocean.

"Yeah," Nomed nodded again, "and I don't think it's doing well. Maybe we should try to catch up with Jack."

"Do you think he's causing all this?" Wanderly asked quietly.

"Maybe," Nomed shrugged, "but whatever dreamed this up has put us into our element. If Jack is that building, we're the cogs, and we've got a job to do. But I'm not sure if we're trying to keep things working or tearing it apart."

"Well," Wanderly giggled, "only one way to find out. Let's go poke it with something."

The two set out at a jog, trying to catch up to Jack, who was now a tiny figure in the distance heading towards a small forest in a valley between the broken mountains. Nomed adjusted the two-handed sword on his back and flexed his magical leather cape into a pair of bat wings and back to a fluttering cloth. He could fly and bypass all the obstacles, but that would mean leaving Wanderly behind. Not that the smaller man couldn't handle himself, but he was a useful tool, even if he was an annoying distraction most of the time.

The world shifted again. It didn't happen with a burst of light, a blurring of everything before settling into reality, or anything else like that. It changed in the blink of an eye, like when you're on a long road and don't remember the past stretch of road going by, and instead you're just in a new place. Nomed thought of it like a dream transition or turning the page of a book.

He didn't like the idea of someone messing with his perception. Reality was supposed to be linear, but now it was hopping, skipping, and jumping to a place where it wanted him to be, which was at the edge of a dark forest. The smells of moist treefalls and rotting undergrowth reached his nose. He could hear scurrying movements in the branches of the canopy above him, and he could taste the thick ground fog winding between the trunks of ancient oaks, maples, and a dozen other trees he couldn't identify.

"Neat!" Wanderly squealed. "How cool was that? One moment we're running—admittedly, not my favorite thing— and the next we're here. And how weird is it that there's a chill wind? Oh, creepy."

"Not neat," Nomed said, his voice barely above a whisper, "and keep your voice down. We need to listen."

Wanderly ran his thumb and pointer across his lips, twisted his hand, and tossed away an imaginary object. "You got it, boss. I'll be quiet as a church mouse. Which is a weird saying, don't you think? Do you think mice in churches are quieter out of respect for the gods, or because they fear a little mousey inquisition?"

"Shush," Nomed hissed, cocking his head.

A small, muffled sound came from just off the path a short way into the trees. Nomed moved forward, Wanderly following, and crept towards the noise. Reaching over his shoulder, he slid the long steel weapon from its scabbard and held it in front of him at the ready. A glance at the halfling showed he held a knife in each hand.

The trees closed around them, and the light fell away, dropping them into a dim, murky circle of fog that trailed around their ankles and trees like snakes made of mist and ill intentions. Sounds echoed eerily. Every step squished from years of fallen leaves and sent up small sprays of grey tendrils which crept away to merge with the surrounding fog.

Approaching the source of the sound, Nomed saw a sliver of a pale face with two wide eyes staring at him. He stopped in his tracks, and Wanderly leaned around his hip to find out why.

"Jack!" the smaller man exclaimed. "Oh, man, you had us freaking out!"

Wanderly paused under Nomed's glare, looking Jack up and down. The man was entangled in the roots of a thick banyan tree, a dozen branches as thick as a man's body looming overhead, and hundreds of roots as thick as a man's finger weaving and tightening around his struggling form.

"Jack?" Wanderly said. "Why's that tree trying to hug you to death? Did you try to build a fire in a haunted forest? Because that would be pretty stupid if you did."

Nomed's heavy blade came down, sliding along the roots and hitting the ground a hairbreadth from Jack's splayed and trapped fingers. Jack let out a startled and muffled screech.

"Stop that," Wanderly snapped. "Now look what you've done. You made the tree hug him harder."

"We need to get him out of there," Nomed spat, "it's killing him."

"I see that, but brute force won't be the way to do it," Wanderly said. "It's going to take distraction and finesse. Let me handle this."

"How the hell do you distract a tree?" Nomed growled.

"Like this." Wanderly twirled his blades and struck them together.

The twin blades made a sharp, piercing chime, then

scraped along one another. Wanderly began whistling as he continued to hammer out a beat and accompanying tune by sliding his blades along one another. He lifted a foot and brought it down on a thick root, using it like a drum and his bare foot as the beater. The tune started out sharp and fast, and over the next few minutes, slowed in pace and lowered in volume. Wanderly swayed and waved his hands, continuing to accompany his whistling with the scraping percussion of his blades. The roots holding their friend relaxed as the music took on a haunting and eerie ease, like a spirit on the wind, finally settling into its daily rest after a hard night of freaking people out.

"Now," Wanderly said out of the corner of his mouth while continuing his song.

"Now, what?" Nomed whispered, jerking out of his own stupor.

"Now brute force," Wanderly said, pacing each word with a thump of his foot on the root. "It's time for your violence."

"Oh," the corners of Nomed's mouth turned down with understanding.

The demon hybrid dipped the tip of his blade and sliced upward at an angle, cutting the despondent roots along the right side of Jack's pale form. He brought it down again on the other side, freeing the man's arms.

The tree burst into movement, cut roots flailing and a hiss like a teakettle rising as sap oozed from the broken tendrils. Wanderly dodged in under Nomed's sword, trailing his twin blades along Jack's legs to cut the restraining hold of the angry botanical giant. Jack surged forward, trying to escape the grasp that moments ago had held him firmly.

Nomed leaned in to cut away anything behind Jack and noted that the roots had been burrowing into his friend. Thin, stunted roots stuck out of Jack's flesh like porcupine quills, each about the length of a finger. Wanderly worked his blades in a whirlwind, shining glints of steel resembling drops of life-giving rain while doing the exact opposite. Nomed's blade was lightning, striking in huge flashes that left gaping holes.

Grabbing Jack under the arms, Wanderly fell to his back,

pulling the man over him and flipping him clear with his feet planted in Jack's gut. Jack tumbled free onto the broken path as Wanderly spun to his feet, still slicing at the roots as Nomed assisted with the thicker branches.

The entire tree shuddered, long sunken roots tearing free of the soft ground and a fetid smell of decomposing vegetation filled the air. Dark insects rose in a thick cloud, choking the three men, and Nomed's cape formed bat wings and, with even strokes, created a wind and blew the miniature attackers back. Jack crawled further away, Wanderly moved to help, and Nomed covering the retreat.

"What do you think of that rescue?" Wanderly chuckled, wiping his blades free of the sticky sap before sheathing them.

"Spiders," Jack croaked.

"What?" Wanderly drew the word out. "That makes no sense."

"He means those," Nomed said, pointing where Jack was looking.

## 5. Why Knot?

Thin threads disappeared into the dark distance, fat drops of gooey dew dancing on them. They were spaced wide apart on the near edge of the crater and drew closer together as they reached the center. Criss-crossing strands created an interlaced lattice of bridges no thicker than a single hair. Dozens of spiders moved along the arachnid highway tending to the dewy droplets, binding or discarding objects that had fallen into the net or on less obvious tasks.

Looking closer, Wanderly noted countless black specks writhing inside the gooey dew. "Hey, neato," Wanderly crowed, pointing at the nearest, "those are egg sacks. I bet there are hundreds of spiders inside each one. And I count at least fifty or sixty sacks before they disappear into the dark. And check this out…"

The small man picked up a leaf on a twig and ran it along a strand of the web. The webbing sliced a neat, thin line into the greenery and one half fluttered away and into the chasm below.

"Razor wire!" Wanderly beamed up at his companions. "I bet it would take off our toes if we tried to sneak across."

"Wanderly," Nomed hissed, looking out across the web, "stop that. Don't touch the web again."

Wanderly followed the man's gaze and saw that every

spider on the web-way had quit whatever it had been doing and all eyes were on him. And there were a lot of eyes.

"Did you guys notice," Jack said, lowering the waterskin he held, "the landscape changed again. We're not in the woods anymore. This is some sort of cavern."

"If this is a cavern," Nomed said, looking up and around, "then I assume those sparkling lights are crystals or something, and not stars embedded in the rock?"

"I think that's safe to say," Jack nodded and took another drink from the waterskin.

"They aren't sparkling," Wanderly giggled. "They'd need a light source to do that. They're twinkling."

"Then what about those inside the crater?" Nomed pointed.

"Um, cosmic cave cobwebs?" Jack suggested.

"Don't be stupid, Jack," Wanderly rolled his eyes. "Cobwebs come from dust collecting, they're not real webs. This would be more like Celestial Spider Center."

"The CSC?" Jack tilted his head. "I think I heard of them. But let's get on with where we are and why."

"There's a tunnel on the other side of the..." Nomed waved his free hand while squinting across the crater, "whatever this is."

"He did say there'd be three trials," Jack muttered, leaning towards where Nomed had indicted and peering, "so I guess this is the second one."

"Who said that, Jack?" Wanderly asked, tilting his head up and to the side, looking at the man askance. "Have you met others here in the basement?"

"It was some guy," Jack explained, "tied me to a chair, asked me questions, attacked my character. You know, things like that."

"First," Nomed interjected.

"What?" Jack asked.

"This is your first trial," Nomed explained.

"No, it isn't." Jack shook his head. "The first was when that tree got me."

"That wasn't a challenge for you, Jack," Nomed said

slowly. "That was for us. So we could catch up, meet with you, and decide if we wanted to help you through this."

Jack chewed on this for a moment before nodding slowly. "Could be. That sounds like something he'd do. I appreciate you deciding to help, though."

"Who is he, Jack?" Wanderly pressed. "We haven't seen anyone else. The only thing we saw was you at a well talking to yourself, and once you ran away, we saw the Inn on a flying island, and it was falling apart. Feels like this might mean something, doesn't it?"

"It feels like it means that the game is afoot," Jack said, as Wanderly exchanged a look with Nomed.

Taking a tentative step forward, Jack touched the tip of his booted foot to the wire webwork and froze. Across the expanse, the spiders silently skittered across the webs towards them. Wanderly gasped in surprise and heard Nomed draw his blade.

Jack sat at a table, swirling a cup of coffee. He studied the little pale brown paper cup and wondered why recycled paper products were more expensive than ones that weren't made from recycled paper. He remembered days when people got paid for bringing in rubber, glass, paper, metals, and other things to be recycled.

"Isn't the saying something like what was old is new again?" he asked aloud.

"Nope," answered a woman with a smoker's voice. "Not anymore, Jack. Now it's 'what's new is old again', because people are shit."

Jack turned in his seat and looked around to see who'd spoken to him. He was in an outdoor café with a table made of interwoven metal and uncomfortable chairs to match. Traffic zoomed by a few paces to one side, with foot traffic between him and the cars. A faded umbrella shaded half the table, but not the half where he sat.

The woman who'd spoken sat at a table in front of him.

She was tattooed, her arms and cleavage a splash of color and half told stories, and her dark hair was shaved on one side and cut short across the rest of her head. She smiled at him, a silver ring shining in her lower lip, matching the hoops climbing her ears. A sweet smell wafted from her as she drew from a short thick cigar in one hand, and she raised her ice coffee towards Jack with her other hand in a toast.

"How'd you know my name?" he asked.

"I don't know your name," she paused, then laughed. "Your name is Jack? Really?"

"Yeah, really," Jack nodded. "I was wondering if we'd met sometime, somewhere."

"Naw, it's just something I call people. So, Jack, what's bothering you? Why were you asking about old and new?"

"Well," Jack rocked his head from side to side with an embarrassed grin, "I was just wondering why we pay more for recycled things. Not old things, mind you. I get why an antique would cost more. Besides the aesthetic of a bygone age, it's nice to have things that stand the test of time."

"Like us?" the woman laughed again. "I often like to think of myself as retro, but not sure if I'm up to being called vintage or antique yet."

"Maybe," Jack frowned, looking at his hands for a long moment, then raised his eyes to study his conversation partner.

She had some age to her, but not a lot. He could see the lines in her face that told him she wasn't in her twenties anymore but could be just into her thirties or as old as almost fifty.

"I've never been very good at judging ages," Jack said, smiling at her.

"Why is that, Jack?" she asked.

"I don't know," he shrugged, "maybe because I travel a lot. Different cultures often seem to be more ageless than one's own."

"What about your own culture?" she asked. "Can you judge someone's age if they're your people?"

"Not really," he shook his head. "I move around so much;

I don't really feel I have a culture that would claim me. And I appreciate other cultures so much that I won't claim one of my own."

Jack trailed off as a big truck trundled by, its steam engine popping and hissing. He squinted after it, wondering where exactly he'd stopped for coffee. He looked up, taking in the details of the surrounding buildings. They were old, but not ancient. Stone instead of concrete and sported columns on the third of six or seven stories. Small, single-passenger vehicles hummed above him, moving between the taller glass towers of buildings in the distance.

The café front was beige brick done in straight angles and boxy design. Canvas awnings stretched away from the building, giving an enclosed and cozy feel to the sidewalk. The buildings on each side of it were done in styles that were a cousin to the café, like they designed the street to show the march of progress and time.

"Pretty interesting place, isn't it?" the woman smiled as she followed his gaze. "I bet that's what triggered your train of thought. The entire city is a mish-mash of times and places. You can take a gas-powered cab to the railplane depot, or grab a rickshaw to the zeppelin towers in midtown."

Jack wanted to ask where he was, but he knew that would be strange. Kind of like every time travel movie when they ask what year it was or grabbing a newspaper to find out the date. If newspapers were still available. But Jack didn't see any advertisement billboards flashing in neon and LED, rotating through a dozen must-have products.

"Interesting is an understatement," Jack mumbled. "It's strange and disconcerting, but familiar at the same time. No matter where I look, something is familiar and sitting beside something that seems out of place."

"Just like anywhere at any given point in time, right?" She grinned. "Life is like that, though. Just when you get your bearings, it throws something at you and kicks your feet out from under you. Why do you think that is?"

Blinking at the question, Jack leaned back and sipped at his coffee. Looking across the table, he saw his pipe pouch sitting beside his half eaten English muffin, the melted butter congealing on a ceramic plate.

"I suppose it's because we crave change and for things to get better and advance, but we love our familiar creature comforts. But for everything that changes, we lose something else."

The woman stood up, her metal chair grinding on the flagstones, picked up her drink and cigar, and moved to Jack's table. She pointed at the empty chair across the table.

"You mind?" she asked. "Would it be okay if I joined you?"

"Feel free," Jack waved at the seat, his lips creasing downward as he shrugged.

"I'm not flirting or trying to get a hook-up, okay?" she said as she set her drink down, noisily pulled out the chair and settled into it.

"Ha." Jack laughed sharply. "I didn't think you were. I'm not that kind of guy. The type that thinks a good conversation means that we're going to—"

Jack let the words trail off, raised his cup to his lips and drank. He reached for his pipe pouch and held it up.

"Do you mind if I smoke too?" he asked with a smile.

"Betty," the woman said with a laugh and held out a hand.

Jack had to juggle the pipe he'd pulled out of the pouch to extend his hand and shake hers.

"Big Bottomed Black Betty is what they call me," she smiled, slowly raising her cigar to take a deep drag before lowering it and blowing out a long stream of thick smoke. "They even named this cigar after me."

"Oh," Jack said, pulling a pinch of tobacco from the pouch and thumbing it into his pipe. "And you don't find that—"

"Offensive?" Betty interrupted, laughing again. "No, not at all. I know what I look like, and I know who I am. Can many people say that, Jack? Do you know who you are?"

"I like to think I do," he said between puffs as he lit his pipe with a gold lighter. "But sometimes I surprise myself with something new."

"Or by clutching to something old and refusing to change when it would be for the better in the long run," Betty said, her voice thick with sarcasm. "I've seen way too many people like that, especially the old white men who run the world."

"Am I an old white man?" Jack asked.

"I don't know, Jack, are you?" Betty leaned back and drew on her cigar. "It's a state of mind, if you know what I mean. I don't mean it as a generalization, but more as a specific vocal minority that happens to hold many positions that allow them to control others through their power. It's bullshit."

"So, we're talking politics?" Jack asked, also leaning back and drawing on his pipe. "I am not prone to arguing for the sake of it. I prefer to have a discussion that can actually cause real change."

"Then change, Jack." She stared at him for a long moment before continuing. "You can be a bull in a china shop. You can be a bully. But it's all just stupid and cowardly if you aren't doing it for the right reasons. Being a simp and bowing out of any confrontation is just as bad if you avoid the hard things just to stay in your comfort zone. Does that make sense to you?"

"You want guys like me to be an asshole?" Jack's voice was tight, sardonic, and his face was neutral.

"I want you to do the right thing, no matter how hard it is, if it helps others. I mean, why can't it be both?"

Jack looked over Betty's shoulder, watching a young woman jogging with a huge dog on a leash as she passed an older woman with a small dog. The older woman struggled for each step, moving slowly, but appearing to be happy to be out and her little yappy dog excitedly sniffing at everything and bouncing from smell to smell.

"I think," Jack pulled on his pipe and exhaled a cloud of smoke, "I see what you mean. Nice guys don't get in control. If they did, they'd make decisions to help others. But they can't be nice guys if they can stomach what must be done to get to that position."

"That sounds about right," Betty nodded. "Are you a nice guy, Jack?"

"I try to be," he shrugged. "I don't like forcing people to my way of thinking. I feel once you do that, you're no longer letting people choose what to do and what they want. You're telling them your way is the right way."

"Is your way the right way?" Betty asked. "Would your ideas help those regular people if you put them through without them wanting it? Would they be better off? And if so, why wouldn't you do it to help them?"

"Well, probably…" Jack mumbled, rubbing his temples with his fingertips.

"Sounds like you're being the asshole by not helping people using your ideas that they'd never come up with, Jack." Betty paused to take a drink, locking her eyes on his.

"I don't think I want to hang out and chat anymore if you're the type of guy who will let others suffer because you might hurt their feelings by doing what they wouldn't. Good luck with that, Hack." Betty stood up, shoving her chair back with her knees. "Because that's what you are if you claim something but won't actually do it."

She turned and weaved through the sidewalk tables and their occupants.

"I don't even know what I did," Jack muttered, "and maybe that's the real problem."


Nomed watched Jack. The man was motionless, one foot touching the web, twitching. He didn't know what his friend was struggling with but wanted to help. The spiders glided along the webs, hundreds of them, threating to overwhelm him and Wanderly. They crawled along the thin stone walkway, the large ones coming one at a time, but the smaller ones like a small flood, washing around their feet.

Wanderly danced. The smaller man literally danced around. Each step crushed a handful of the smaller arachnids, as he chose a partner from the dog-sized creatures. He whistled and sang, the words and tune interweaving like a web of its own, confusing the creatures long enough to take one or two out with his knives.

Nomed focused on the larger beasts, his sword sliding

through the bulbous, hairy abdomens of the attackers. He was good at this, but it frustrated him he couldn't get to the source. A way to attack the puppet master in the center of the web, and strike at the heart of the problem.

"Wanderly," Nomed shouted, "take care. I'm going to strike at the heart of the attack."

"Wha—" was all Wanderly was able to say before Nomed launched himself into the air and across the chasm, his leather cloak billowing into bat-like wings.

The demon-spawn glided crookedly across the space, lashing out at spiders crossing the webs towards his friend. He reached the shining center of the web, and a massive, glowing form sat there. Landing atop the creature, he stabbed down into the beast's abdomen. His sword slid easily into the hairy, bulbous segment. White and red ichor oozed out of the wound, and thousands of hissing screams came from all around.

A gong sounded. It shook the demon-spawn, causing his head to spin. It was unnerving and disorienting as the sound echoed back and forth, and he couldn't be sure if it was in his head or across the cavernous space. Nomed felt his footing go out from under him. Launching himself back into the air, his leathery wings struggled to keep him aloft as he wobbled. Lilting to one side, he struck repeatedly at what he thought of as the queen of the nest.

The creature screamed and the throng of spiders threatening to overwhelm Wanderly stopped as one and turned towards the center of the web. In a unified surge, they turned towards Nomed and rushed forward. He watched, slashing at the boss, and clenched his sphincter as the spindly wave of attackers washed over him.

## 6. Meanwhile, Hack at the Inn

Croaker watched as another stone fell from the misty amber sky, landing in an empty space between two others on the slowly growing wall. It was expanding as well; the length extending outside the perimeter of the tent that was once an inn.

"I don't know if those damned stones are sinking or burrowing," Croaker muttered to no one in particular.

"Well, it must form the basement," Elementius said. "After all, we do have various and sundry people down there. And I assume we'd like to be able to retrieve them."

Croaker looked from the wall to the pudgy man. *He is pudgy*, he thought. *It's like he's expanding his boundaries as the Inn expands its own.*

"But what is it using to do it?" Croaker asked. "Why are stones falling from the sky?"

"You're asking excellent questions, Master Norge," the professor replied, speaking as if Croaker were a first-year student. "This plane is a very special place and made from the very fibers of creativity. All of which are mined from a very singular source that is unique in and of itself when compared to everything else in the universe."

The scholar stared out the window, a look of longing and awe twisting his face. "It's like he never realized…"

Elementius whispered and trailed off.

"It's like who never realized what, ya windbag?" Croaker barked. "Don't leave us hanging. You know we're listening. Don't act like you don't."

Croaker gestured to the people assembled in the room. Tilbert sat at a table with Mogits and Tiffene, their heads drawn close together as they discussed something they didn't want overheard. Manx sat with Kitty and Fritz, the smaller man in his were-Pomeranian form reenacting a battle, much to Kitty's delight and amusement. Sam leaned on the wall, leaning over to peer outside into the eternal sunset. Golem tided up the mantle on the newly grown fireplace, which was twice as wide as the automaton's outspread arms.

"Jack, that's who," Elementius said. "It's like he never realized how much his abilities extended. The man thinks he travels through time and space, but I don't think he realizes he travels through much more than that. It's not my bailiwick, you grouchy codger, but are you familiar with basic quantum physics?"

"No, I am not." Croaker said, his tone sharp. "And you shouldn't be familiar with it, either. You come from a world that deals in magic, not science."

"Oh, you poor fool," Elementius smirked. "I am not from the world of Aetheria. Neither from the time period Jack hails from, the era Manx and Mogits lived in, nor the later years which Sam and Tiffene hails from, which would be the same you lived in. I am from elsewhere, drawn here by Jack and his needs. But what you don't seem to comprehend is that Jack has layers. Many layers, but some are more dominant than others."

The professor paused, lifting his drink from the stone table in front of him. That made Croaker do a double take. That table had been wooden slats last he looked. Things were changing in the inn faster than he could follow.

"The Jack you know, the one you see every day," Elementius continued, "is just one aspect of himself. He's been working on more than just what you see. You may recall him disappearing for hours or days and returning looking different. Maybe a change of clothes. Maybe the growth of facial hair. Perhaps looking gaunter and more drawn. It isn't always the same Jack that returns. And I know that we're all constantly changing, but in his case, it's much more literal and much more expansive than how we're altered by events."

Professor Elementius looked into Croaker's eyes and smiled a knowing smile. With a flourish, he asked, "Are you keeping up? You're a creative soul who can cobble together amazing things from different and unrelated items to create something new and different. Can you see how a soul could do that also?"

"A soul?" Croaker scoffed. "Now we're talking about metaphysics? People transforming into someone new?"

"Yes." Elementius slammed an open palm down on the table. "Wonderful, you get it. Jack's aspects change when he returns. He's not the same man. He's a version of himself, but not the same version who left moments or weeks before."

"What…" Croaker slowed and stopped before taking a drink, his glass now a thick crystal. "What are you getting at?"

"Ah," Elementius sighed, but while grinning a superior grin, his eyes dancing with mischief. A fold of fat made his eyes look piggish, and he went on, looking down his short and upturned nose, "You don't get it. That's sad, which is why you're outdone and useless. Jack has come back too many times as someone slightly different. The multiverse, my limited and dense friend, I am speaking of the countless and myriad worlds through which he travels."

The room had fallen silent. Every group of people had stopped talking amongst themselves and now watched the two and listened to the oddly disjointed conversation. Croaker shook his head, as if trying to shoo away a biting insect.

"I'm…" Croaker stopped, lifting his empty glass to drink and staring at it stupidly, then said, almost to himself, "I'm not stupid. I understand what you're saying. But that couldn't have changed Jack so much that this should happen."

The older man waved at the reconstruction, then towards the bar. Where he sat no longer held a bar. Instead, was a long stone counter that looked more like an alchemist's lab, but holding bottles and kegs of alcohol. He reached over and took a greenish bottle. Popping the cork, he poured amber liquid into his glass. He set the bottle down, lifted the glass to his lips, then stopped. Looking over the rim of the glass at Elementius, he lowered it to the counter, feeling it may be best if he didn't imbibe. Though he sorely wanted to. It changed. It could be poison, or it could be whiskey.

*Not much difference when you need your wits about you*, he thought.

Elementius waited patiently, letting the man process his thoughts, but smirked again as he took another drink from his own glass.

"Why?" Croaker asked vaguely. "Why would Jack allow himself to be changed?"

"He wouldn't," Elementius said, looking at the ceiling, "at least not consciously. But within him is so much more, just waiting to be activated. He needed to go through very specific experiences to cause these changes. He knew this but would never admit it to his conscious mind. Thus, he drew others here to replace the ones holding him back."

A noise of scraping metal from behind him made Croaker jerk to look over his shoulder, like a child who'd just listened to a scary tale around the campfire.

Golem moved from the fireplace to what was once the bar and held Cogsley's arm, thrusting the limb into his midsection. The metal scraping was the sound of Cogsley's body be drug across the stone floor and being absorbed into Golem's body. The clay construct's body now had a distinctive masculine look, and a distant—almost rapturous—look on his changing face.

"What the hell are you doing?" Croaker shouted, jumping from the stool to his feet. He spun towards the two automatons and took a step forward.

"Uh, uh, uh," Elementius said, his voice rising in pitch with each syllable. "I wouldn't interfere. The others Jack summoned here may have something to say about it."

Croaker glanced over his shoulder and saw every person—barring Elementius and Tilbert—had drawn a weapon. Metal and magic gleamed in every hand. Mogits held a blue globe, ready to be launched. Manx had his twin daggers out. Tiffene's arms had iced over to the elbow, Sam standing behind and to one side of her with six-shooters drawn. Fritz was on top of the one remaining wood-plank table, with Kitty standing beside him, her arm cannon ready and a wounded look on her face. Darome was wide-eyed but held an amorphous blob wavering in front of him. Durg had balled his fists and crouched, moving closer to Croaker but facing to the others in the room. Tilbert typed on his floating stenographer's machine, looking sad but full of conviction.

"You're the old guard, Croaker." Elementius leaned back, crossing thick arms across his expansive midsection. "You and the gnome and the half-breed ogre. Wanderly and Nomed will be dealt with in turn. Perhaps to join us, perhaps to be sent away or destroyed, but either way, they will join us or die. Out with the old and in with the new. You are each blocking progress. You are the enemy if you refuse to allow Jack to metamorphosis into what he's becoming."

"And what's that?" Croaker asked, looking from the slowly disappearing bartender to the fat man.

"There's a war coming," Elementius said, "and we need to change to be able to fight it. Jack has mentioned this numerous times. He called it a storm sometimes and referred to it in other ways at times. He wasn't even sure what was coming, but his other self—or selves—recognized what needed to be done. This is all Jack's doing, and he doesn't even know it."

Elementius laughed, but it was a bitter sound as he looked down at his new girth.

"Don't you see?" the professor went on, "It's already well on the way. We're all changing. It's only picked up speed now that Jack is in the final stages."

Croaker looked down at his own body, then at Darome and Durg.

"Not everyone is changing," he growled. He gestured at himself, then the gnome and half-ogre, "We're not changing. And we'll stand in your way until Jack comes back and sets things right."

"Why not wait until he does?" Elementius said with a small

laugh and raised eyebrows. "If you think he'd want you to live and help him further, just let the inn reconstruct itself to what he wants it to be. You've never interfered before. Why start now?"

"Because I don't think he'd want these changes," Croaker barked, "and I'm confident that the four of us can hold you eight off until he returns."

"Three of you," a voice said from behind Croaker, causing him to turn. "And there's nine of us, sir."

Golem stood behind him, Cogsley's legs slowly sliding into the clay construct's body. The creature had a much more defined look now that he'd absorbed the previous keeper of the inn. A new being stood where the two had been a few moments before. Instead of a clumpy, bulky, misshapen creature, Golem was tall and straight, clothed in all black. He wore a fine suit stretched across a massive chest, a thin red tie bright against the midnight blue dress shirt underneath. He was a muscle-bound hulk in a refined outfit, cracking thick knuckles in front of his toned and shaped torso. Glassy eyes showed small brass pieces behind them, and his smile showed too many shiny, golden teeth.

Croaker took a step back, even as Darome launched himself bodily at the renewed, living mannequin. Golem caught the gnome by the head and held him at arm's length. Durg surged forward, a blur of violence, fists coming in low below the gnome to thud uselessly in rapid succession into the thing's midsection. Golem raised Darome up, and slapped the half-ogre with the gnome's feet, Darome screaming in pain as he did.

"Continue your fruitless attack," Golem said, "and I shall beat you to death with your friend even as he dies."

"Durg, stop," Croaker shouted, "this isn't going to work!"

Croaker looked behind him at Elementius and looked straight down the barrel of Kitty's arm cannon.

"Kitty?" the older man whispered.

"I'm sorry, boss," Kitty whispered back. "I know. I know what I've been through, and I promised myself I'd never be on the losing side again. I promise you now that I'll do everything to keep them in line and on the level, but this is Jack's place. I don't know why I was brought here, but I know I don't want to hurt you."

Croaker tried to turn to face her and let out a cry of pain of his own. Looking down, he saw his legs had been frozen in place to the stone floor, ice extending up to his knees. His arthritis stabbed, and he wobbled, then tumbled over. He lay on the floor, staring up at Tiffene grimly staring down at him, and Fritz, in full furry fury, glaring at him. The woman looked sad, as if she had to put a beloved pet down.

"Don't Durg," Manx muttered from beside Mogits, who now held blue glowing ethereal daggers. "Mogits will cut beyond bone with those daggers of his. He will cut your soul. You're a sweet man, Durg. And I'd hate to see you hurt, or your friend."

"Or filled with lead," Sam harrumphed, his twin pistols held at arm's length and pointed at the big man's head.

"If I may," Golem said, "I'd prefer to be called Victavalen now, meaning unstoppable strength. That would be a viable definition for me in your time. Isn't that correct, Kitty?"

"I think so," Kitty shrugged, "but it's hard to think about that when we're living in a reality where men have the power to change everything."

"Croaker," Elementius said, "call we say this round is over? You're on the floor, and your friends face even more dire responses if they continue."

"Yes, yes," Croaker barked. "I've already told them to stop. You've got the upper hand, and there's not much for us to do besides die. For now."

The last two words were a muttered whisper.

"I have excellent hearing," Elementius said, ' but we shall call this exchange over. Victavalen, put the gnome down. Tiffene, thaw the old man. They're powerless now, anyway."

"Of course, sir," the newly remade automator said, dropping Darome into a crumpled heap on the floor.

Durg dropped to his knees, kneeling in front of Victavalen to gently scoop his friend up, supporting the gnome's neck. Croaker couldn't help but notice that it looked like the half-ogre was submitting to a new master.

Croaker shuddered with the implications, his hand resting inside his duster and clutching the papers hidden within. He hoped they would be enough to fix things. Or at least stop them from completely going to shit.

## 7. At Death's Door

Nomed hacked at the spiders, moving with a blinding speed he couldn't maintain for long. The astral arachnids would overwhelm him soon if something didn't turn up to help him. There are master swordsmen and then there is Nomed. The man was raised with a blade in his hand. Not by his adoptive parents' choice, but by his own decision. It was more of his rebellious nature, and something to balance the book lessons, explorations into strategy, and moral conundrums.

That last thing what was he failed at the most often, usually on purpose. He excelled at the strategy sessions and knew the right answers in the study of right and wrong. He just never saw the purpose of always making the right choice. It wasn't always the most beneficial, or the most interesting.

Swooping on the magical leather wings formed of his cape, he sliced through the shimmering silken ropes the spiders used as a footpath as easily as any person would use a road. The creatures were the same inky onyx as the abyss in front of Nomed and Wanderly, almost invisible. Even his demon-inherited vision that allowed him to see in most conditions was of little use. But it was something, and it let him see their myriads of glinting eyes moving against the background of distant stars.

He cut away the strands closest to Jack but couldn't move

too far away without risking others getting to the rocky ledge Wanderly danced back and forth upon. The small man was stomping and clapping, trying to draw the attention of spiders to distract them. Then the small man let out a cry of eureka and began whistling.

Nomed had heard many people whistle a tune, but Wanderly had a gift like no other he'd ever seen or heard. The melody leapt forward from him and the spiders hesitated. Nomed was unsure if they were listening, or if the sounds dazed and confused them. A deep throaty beat followed, and a second thread of whistling joined the first to create a harmony that wove around the melody. The creatures wavered, and a half dozen lost their footing and fell, twisting as they disappeared into the depths. Others stopped completely, quivering, while some of the closest tried to backpedal and climb over the stunned ones to retreat.

"I don't know what you're doing, Wanderly," Nomed shouted, "but I think it's helping. A lot."

The clapping and stomping returned, joining the bass beat from the little man, the winding melody and twisting harmony interweaving like an auditory web of the wee man's making.

The stars in the far distance began winking out like watching eyes closing or withdrawing to a further distance before disappearing completely.

Nomed slashed at the nearest spiders, knocking them from their precarious perches and into the hungry darkness. He glanced back and saw Jack wavering like a heat mirage in the desert. The entire scene began melting and Nomed felt his gorge rise. Like a painting in the sun, reality dripped down the sides of the man's peripheral vision. Nomed dove for firm ground, his own equilibrium becoming unstable. Landing with a crash, Nomed rolled to his feet, dizzy and disoriented.

Shaking his head to clear it, the world shifted, and the two stood alone on a dark, rocky plain. No sun or stars were in the sky, but an eerie dim light showed the same scene as far as Nomed could see.

"Where's Jack?" came Wanderly's voice, and the small man swam into focus. "Uh oh, I think we've lost him again."

He'd summoned the crows. Jack didn't know how he'd done it, but he had. He held his coffee cup as he gazed into the burnished sunset sky at a flock of twenty or thirty dark harbingers circling overhead, calling in a series of two or three caws. More were in the tall autumn grass around him, and he could hear others in the dark line of trees in the distance.

*Danger,* Jack thought, *that's what that means to these tribes in this area. And why am I thinking of them as a tribe? Isn't a flock of crows a murder?*

But he knew, somehow, that crows didn't think in human terms. They thought of themselves as a tribe. At least that was as close to the term that fit in the human tongue. He'd never called crows before. The thought had never even crossed his mind, certainly not while sitting in a sidewalk café.

*But I'm not in a café,* he realized, *at least not anymore. The world has changed again.*

He no longer held a coffee cup. Instead, he gripped a walking stick that came to his shoulder. He was dressed in his traveling clothes, a simple affair of browns and beiges, each piece sturdy and well used. In the tree line, he could see the jittering lights of oil lamps shining dimly through windows.

He moved towards them, realizing the sun was setting and the horizon beyond the trees was the deep purple of oncoming night. He passed a scarecrow raised high on a wooden pole, its empty eyes staring down at him. It was dressed in the same fashion as him, but with small differences. Looking across the knee-high grasses, he noticed dozens of others similarly dressed, all of them facing him.

Picking up his pace, the longhouse in front of him, he studied it. It was a tavern like ones he'd seen in the northern lands not long ago. Made of logs with mud between, it stretched the length of five farmhouses and was low to the ground. Windows dotted the structure, each about waist high, and he realized the building was partially sunken into the wet earth. A fog had risen, and swirls danced around his feet with each step. The temperature had also dropped, and he could see his breath in front of him in small puffs.

"Moors and the forest are cousins that stare at each other across the fence of the darkened night," he muttered.

Stopping in front of the building, he saw three entrances, each down a short flight of stone steps. Leathery wings rustled overhead in the dark, the amber cat's-eye moon not giving enough light to tell what the sound belonged to, but enough to make the ground fog glow with a haunting luminescence. The sound came again, this time from two directions at once.

He moved to the center door, the other two too far to the left and right to consider using. He carefully descended the four slick steps, thick with moss, and raised a fist to the stout oaken door. The door creaked open a hand-span before he could knock. With a shrug, Jack pushed it open and entered.

It took a few moments for his eyes to adjust. Wide wooden tables stretched in both directions, benches lining each side. A half dozen figures sat at the closest tables, murky and indistinct, like in a dream. The shadowy forms sat in ones and twos, hunched over wooden trenchers, drinking from wooden mugs, or smoking long clay pipes. Near a dwindling fire in a massive stone hearth sat a single man at a smaller square table. He looked up, squinting at Jack, and smiled, showing a mouth with more than a few gaps. The man was old and dark of skin and gave off a feeling of familiarity and cunning. He gestured to an empty chair across the table with the stem of his pipe.

"Join me, Jack," the man said. "The night is cold and long here, and I don't expect sleep will be visiting for a long while yet."

Moving to take the offered seat, Jack saw a place had been set for him. A sturdy metal tankard sat beside a crockery plate and a wooden bowl. Pulling out the sturdy ladder-back chair, he glanced around the room again now that his eyes had adjusted. The figures he'd seen before were in different seats, or different people were in the same seats. It all slid from one perception to another, people shifting like time-dilated shadows.

"Everything alright, Jack?" the man asked, drawing Jack's

attention back to him.

"What?" Jack turned back to the table and dropped into the chair. "Oh, yeah. Everything's fine. Just looking at the room, it's interesting."

"Take a moment," the man said, leaning back and sticking the pipe back into his mouth. "Look around and get settled before we get down to business."

The interior of the building matched the exterior with dark woods and thick logs used as decorative floor-to-ceiling beams carved in the shape of the local animals—not quite a totem, but similar in design—and long sideboards or benches along the walls. The air was thick with moisture, the hanging wisps of pipe smoke, and the black tendrils of whale oil smoke from the lanterns. The smells combined with the cooking to make a dismal and musty smell with a nutty undertone.

Dusty wood carvings draped with cobwebs sat in recessed alcoves throughout the room and put Jack in mind of a sepulcher and the remembrances people place when remembering those gone before. They were various animals mostly, but an occasional bust sat in between deer, bears, and other forest creatures.

A crow called from a rafter overhead and Jack looked up to see a single ebony bird tilting its head as it studied him with a beady black eye, it sleek shoulders hunkered around its smooth head. It danced from one foot to the other, then crowed once more with a bobbing motion.

"What is this place?" Jack murmured, then turned back to the man across the table.

"It's just a place," the man answered. "We're on the edge of the Shady Wood just south of the Lonely Hills, about two days' travel from Talismont on the Sea of Seron. Bridgemont is the closest large city to the north, if you would consider it large, and it's almost a week away. These lodges are set up about a day's travel apart, so folks don't need to stay the night in the Wood. Few would care to slumber with the spirits and gaunts that haunt such a place."

"I know some of those places," Jack nodded, noticing the lumpy stew of potatoes and greasy meat in the bowl, and the boiled carrots, bread, and oily cheese on his plate.

"I'd hope so, Jack," the man laughed. "After all, you're the one that came to us."

A chill ran down Jack's back and arms as he saw the tankard slowly fill with a watery ale, without anyone pouring it. It was accompanied by a smell, sour and biting, and bits of trub bobbed to the top before slowly sinking into the murk of the drink.

"I don't recognize you, but you know me?" Jack asked, rubbing his elbows and upper arms, despite being near the fire.

"I'm Phil," the man said, waving away the question, "and we all know you here, though the others may not know it. They're all wrapped up in their own problems and caught up with their own thoughts and worries. What's your worries, Jack?"

Jack paused, leaning back a little and clenching his jaw. Whether in frustration or due to the passing chill, he couldn't be sure.

"Did that crow follow me in, or was it always here?" Jack asked after a moment.

"You brought her in with you," Phil grunted, sounding displeased. "We don't favor her kind here. But you're a guest, and we'll let her be if she behaves. It bodes ill, because crows often are harbingers of death, and we get enough of that without them coming around."

"Aren't crows often?" Jack asked, but Phil cut him off.

"Do you really want to talk about crows, Jack?" he said, his voice a harsh hiss. "She's your business. Whether she's your pet, your master, or your guide, that's between you and her. Now, again Jack, I ask you; what do you want to talk about? What are your worries?"

"Where's my friends?" Jack asked impulsively.

"Your friends," Phil said in a whisper, leaning back and glancing towards the door. "I don't know where you left them, but you've been calling them to you, collecting them, haven't you? Are you some sort of warlock, witch, or wizard building a coven? Is that what brought you here?"

Jack wrinkled his forehead and looked at the man from

under his furrowed brows.

"What do you mean?" Jack asked. "I'm just a traveller and happened upon your tavern as the sun set."

"Yes, as the sun set," Phil muttered, "across the field of the guardians, and headed towards where two of your friends are in Talismont."

Jack looked perplexed again.

"The barbarian and the sneak thief who you summoned, Torrents and the Kid," Phil spat into the fire, which hissed and flared as if the spittle had been some flammable liquid. "Do you deny knowing them?"

"No, I don't deny it," Jack said with a bit too much force, "but I didn't know they were here. I thought they were somewhere in the north, near the Common Wood across the Rolling Mountains."

"And the two following you, the demon ilk and his small companion, Nomed, and Wanderly? Do you deny they are your creatures?"

"They're..." Jack hesitated, feeling off balance from the sudden interrogation. "They're not *my creatures*, they're my friends."

"That's four, five, including you, and you have others, don't you?" Phil pressed. "Are you aiming for that magical number of thirteen gathered to do your secretive spells and dark business?"

Jack jerked back, and he thought of the others at the Traveller's Inn. *How many regulars were there? Croaker, Darome, and Durg must count. But the others were new, and he hadn't drawn them there. They had shown up on their own and decided to stay. Didn't they?*

"I think your silence speaks loudly and reveals much," Phil nodded and looked at his pipe, which was no longer clay, but a wrinkled grey wood. "And you travel the ancient ways that were shut down after the age of mages. Now you search the paths of the dead to find more. Who do you seek, necromancer?"

"No," Jack shook his head, "I don't deal with the dead or undead. Yes, I can travel, but I don't need the portal system."

"You admit to travelling, and don't deny the rest. But you've opened them again, haven't you? These doors to realms are forbidden." Phil accused. "They were closed, forgotten and lost in the mists of legends for a reason, Jack. And you're denying shattering ancient covenants and breaking millennia old oaths for your own ends? Do you know what can happen once they're fully open again?"

"Yes," Jack's voice rose, "I know what can happen. Trade among free people, the mixing of cultures, and the sharing of knowledge with people who might never meet."

"And the demons and devils that can use them? What of them, sorcerer?" Phil pressed. "Things from faraway lands that seek to return here to ravage the land and its people? Strange beings that only know darkness once used these things you say can help. Every soul in here had fallen prey to such things, and now you return to this place to what? Bring us under your power? Control us and use us for your dark machinations?"

Jack felt the room darken more than he saw it. The light from the oil lamps dimmed in an oppressive cloud of something he'd rarely felt. He turned to look, and dozens of shadowed forms hunched behind him, just out of the ring of firelight. The crow barked three sharp caws, and the beings wavered and took a step back.

"I think I should be going now," Jack said, standing.

"But you haven't had any of your food or drink," Phil said, suddenly friendly again. The man smiled, but his eyes remaining intense and sharp. "You don't want to go out into the wood at this hour. It would be much better if you stayed. We welcomed you and only want to help you realize the folly of your plans."

Jack looked around him again, sweeping across the body of the shades to stop at an alcove of carved relics on the mantles. He started as he noticed a bust that bared a striking resemblance to him, and words carved below it. Four lines of script resembling an epitaph were clear:

*The task accomplished,*

*The long day done,*
*Let us cross over the river,*
*and rest under the shade of the trees.*

Jack turned and ran for the door he'd entered, the crow launching herself to lead the way. The shadowy forms faded from in front of him and reappeared beside and behind him. Thin, bony hands covered in drawn yellowed flesh reached for him. Moans like whispers of memory wrapped around his mind, and his thoughts became blurred. Jerking the door open, he burst into a cold foggy night, rushed into a man, bounced backwards and tripped. Falling on his butt, Jack's head thudded on the ground, and he slid into the warm, welcoming, and waiting darkness.

## 8. Forward Momentum

"It looks like he was running for his life," Wanderly leaned around Nomed to look at Jack laying in the wet grass, and the small man giggled.

"I think he may have been doing exactly that," Nomed said, hands on hips, his broad chest and muscled arms covered with the small scales that almost never showed, "and I'm not sure how it turned out."

"Do you think he's being chased?" Wanderly asked, squinting into the tree line. "I mean, he came out of nowhere, but it didn't look like he travelled. He was just here. I've seen him travel often enough, and though it's not flashy—well, not most of the time, I've seen the blue archway he makes for others,"

"Chased isn't the right word, more like pursued or haunted. And you're prattling," Nomed interrupted. "But everything you said was relevant."

"Then it wouldn't be prattling, would it?" Wanderly smugly smirked. "If I were prattling, I'd have told you about my Aunt Petunia and why she was called Petunia when her birth name was Keniveve Taria Woddlesnot. Okay, so her last name wasn't Waddlesnot, I just made that up to see if you were listening, because really, Waddlesnot? I mean, it's not like Aunt Petunia was related in the least the Waddlesnot's of Winespit

Valley, right?"

"Yes," Nomed interjected while Wanderly took a breath.

"What?" Wanderly said, knocked off his train of thought, and he knew the conductor would be laughing at him.

"Yes, to all of it. You're right," Nomed went on, "especially about that being prattling compared to the previous statements, but also about the relationship between your aunt and the Winespit Waddlesnots."

"Oh, right?" Wanderly jammed his hands into his pockets and looked around.

Moments ago, the two had been standing in a field bordering a large wood or a small forest. *I wonder what the difference is,* Wanderly wondered, *I mean, when does it get too big to be a wood and magically transform to a forest? And do different animals move into it when it gets the upgrade? And monsters too?*

He stopped, realizing he should share all these thoughts with Nomed. He turned to his friend, who was holding up a finger to forestall anything Wanderly had to say.

"Notice the trees and fields are gone?" Nomed asked in a low voice. "We're back to the rocky wasteland where everything is dark grey or black. I'm beginning to think Jack is controlling where we are. Every time he leaves—physically or mentally—this is where we end up."

"Oh, yeah!" Wanderly chirruped. "I was going to mention that, but then I began wondering about the forest and the woods and when one becomes—"

"Can you please try to stick to the topic?" Nomed sighed the words out.

"Oh, Nomed," Wanderly put his fists on his hips, scrunched up his face in a sour imitation of Nomed, and looked up at his friend, "you sound frustrated. You never know when what I'm saying could be important and pertinent to the topic."

"Once again, you're right." Nomed looked meaningfully at Wanderly. "I *never* know when what you're saying could be important."

"There ya go," Wanderly grinned.

"I'm tired of all this," Jack mumbled from his back

between the two, his eyes still closed.

"He's awake!" Wanderly called.

"Thank you for screeching the obvious, Wanderly," Nomed said, then looked down at Jack. "Tired of us arguing?"

"No," Jack shook his head slowly, then raised his hand to rub his temples with a groan. "Well, that too. But I meant this running from wherever this person keeps sending me. I think it's time to become more proactive, instead of reactive."

Wanderly looked at the study that had appeared around them. Jack sat in a large leather chair behind a massive wooden desk that held a black blotter, an ink well beside a sheaf of parchment, and a laptop computer. Floor-to-ceiling shelves lined the walls, leather-bound books neatly organized with various brass doodads and thingamabobs set between or in front of the tomes. A large globe the size of a water barrel sat in an oak and brass holder; the lands and oceans represented shifted as it faded from one world to another.

Nomed stood over Jack's right shoulder wearing the usual accoutrement of bastard sword and leather cape on his back, but also a tabard with a compass embroidered on it. Looking down, Wanderly took in his own clothes with a snurfle. He wore jester's motley, along with a wicked looking curved black blade on his hip.

"Where is this, then?" Nomed asked, shifting to look at his outfit and the room.

"If this adversary says I can create worlds," Jack said, picking up a stemmed crystal glass that hadn't been there a moment before and taking a drink before continuing, "and keeps sending me to worlds and places of their choosing, then it's long overdue for me to create the places I want to be."

"So, you made an entire world?" Wanderly said wonderingly.

"No," Jack shook his head, "In a very bold and daring move, I made my sanctum where I can think for a few minutes without being accosted by whatever this other person keeps sending at me."

"And where is that?" asked Nomed.

"We're in the Traveller's Inn, of course," Jack turned to

look at Nomed with a grin, his tone both mocking and mischievous. "We're on a floor yet to be built, and once it is, I'll just loop the reality to keep this room between now and then."

"And what's this globe, then?" Wanderly asked. "Is it the world you made?"

"Kind of. That globe represents the world—or worlds— I've visited or will be visiting in the near future," Jack said, turning back in his chair to look across the room at the shimmering artifact. "The same way I've timed the shifts in the portal network on Aetheria; the shifts between realities on that globe have been timed to match. Or timelines, worlds, dimensions, or whatever term you prefer to use. I'm going to need to make a few stops, but first I need to get you two into position."

"Jack," Nomed said, stepping from behind the chair to walk along the bookshelves, trailing a finger in the dust that should have taken months to accumulate, "you're displaying some new abilities. I don't know how I should feel about that."

"Feel however you like, Nomed," Jack sighed. "These aren't new abilities. I've had them all along. At least, I think I did. I'm just looking at ways I've used my skills previously and stretching a bit. Going to the next level, taking the next logical step."

"Oh, logic," Wanderly exclaimed. "That's not something we rely on very much. So, where's this logic leading us next, Jack?"

"First," Jack said, leaning back and putting both of his black booted feet up on the desk and his hands interlinked behind his head, "I need to place both of you. I promise not to compromise either of you or your sensitive moral compasses. I'll place you where you can create chaos and unbalance systems that have been in place. Does that sound okay?"

Wanderly, noting the sarcastic tone in Jack's voice, turned his head back and forth between Nomed and him. Jack's mouth turned up at one corner as he watched the demon-kin. Nomed watched Jack out of the corner of his eye as he moved along the shelves across the room from the desk. Wanderly also noticed the tchotchkes, bric-à-brac, and knickknacks appearing, disappearing, and changing forms and places on the shelves.

"Okay, I'm done," Jack said, standing with an exasperated sigh. "You're my friend, not my boss or a judge and jury. If you don't like how I guide the ride, I can let you off wherever you like. Otherwise, it's time for you to go to the floors below and get things in hand for my return."

"You're returning, Jack?" Nomed asked, turning to face the man behind the desk. "Where are you going, *Jack*?" Nomed leaned into the last word.

"This is the last question you get to ask me, *Nomed*," Jack mimicked the cambion's tone, stepping around the desk and across the room until he was within reach of Nomed. "I'm going to travel through time and space. I am going to set up multiple events, many of which will have a cascading effect and create circumstances I shall take advantage of. Imagine what you do, but on a much greater scale. Now, it's time to go."

Jack pressed a single finger to Nomed's chest and pushed. It was hardly enough for to make the man flinch, but the demon half-breed flew backwards and into a rift that opened behind him. Jack then turned to look at Wanderly.

"Do *you* have any questions?" Jack asked the small man.

"Just one," Wanderly said, caution tinting his tone.

"Well, what is it?" Jack asked with an exasperated sigh.

"Are we still friends?" Wanderly grinned up at Jack, looking like a hungry child who smells of baking cookies.

"Yeah," Jack pushed out a flood of breath while rolling his eyes, "sure, Wanderly."

"Shake on it," Wanderly said with a triumphant crow to his voice, reaching out to take the bigger man's hand with both of his own and pump three times in measured and precise movements before jerking his hands back.

"Ow, what the hell?" Jack bit back further words and looked at three long furrows of curled flesh on the back of in the shape a 'W'. "You scratched me, you little bastard!"

"Oh, did I?" Wanderly made a mock gasp, covering the 'O' of his mouth. Then, grinning, he wiggled his fingers in a goodbye gesture, and said, "I'll show myself out."

Throwing himself backwards as Jack reached to grab him, Wanderly fell through a rift, leaving Jack to wonder if it was the one he was about to create or if the little man could make his own.

"No, impossible," Jack muttered to himself, rubbing the three scratches. "He never did that before. Why would he start now?"

He walked around the room, which was larger than when the three had first arrived. The tower was growing in leaps and bounds, expanding in all dimensions: height, width, depth, time, and more. He could feel it connecting to his preferred times and places. He felt it anchor into the Highest Spire and its myriads of doors throughout the multiverse, and he was glad he'd began that expansion tens of thousands of years ago when the Large Hadron Collider came online on the border of two long-forgotten countries.

It was all planning and legwork he'd done long ago and far away. Now it was time to go back and set other things in motion, and bring back anchors to each spot in time. He'd have to go back further than the inception of the machine that brought the birth of ways-between-worlds. That would take some effort, but he'd done it before and would do it again. He'd gone as far back as—what was it?—700 C.E. in that particular reality. He'd try for that again. It should be enough.

Then it would be back to the tavern below, where the others waited. He'd once thought of many of them as friends, but recent revelations had changed his point of view. They were pawns at best. Perhaps minions if they wanted to play along. But even if they weren't, he'd tell them what not to do, so they'd do what he wanted out of misguided rebellion.

He'd played this game for thousands of years across 70,000 years of a single planet, a planet which had changed so drastically it was now a different reality. It was like moving from the year he was born to prehistoric times when dinosaurs roamed. It was such a different world with continent shifts and the composition of the air breathed, and a hundred other ways that it was a different world.

Not that there wasn't a place on the current timeline where dinosaurs existed. He'd known about the toxic-cloud enveloped land that was surrounded by coral reefs of immense scope and scape. He also knew about the archipelago, which rose from the ocean that still harbored long-forgotten technologies that were so ancient that even myth and legend had forgotten about it. Of course, it had. Civilization had been blasted back to the bronze age, but with the advantage of straggler technology that could be scavenged. It was the troöds trying to get their people home—and when they couldn't, setting off a series of tectonic manipulators, as well as a few bacterial cleanup colonies—who brought about the end of the world as people knew it. In fact, maybe that would be the first place he visited. There was a one Byron Savage that needed a nudge or three.

## 9. Inn-deed and Out-ward

Nomed appeared in the center of what looked like a bar fight, if bar fights included scatterguns, levitating globes of light flying of their own accord, and giant lobster men. The latter was just outside the curved outer wall of the tower.

"What the fuck is a tower doing here?" he muttered.

Quickly looking around, he picked out a few familiar details, but in general everything was different. Last time he was here, it was a cyberpunk rave warehouse with neon and lasers. Before that, it was a cozy tavern or an old west saloon or something.

Now, crustaceans who looked like they bred with centaurs were attacking with wide, flat firearms launching coin-sized disks in a widening dispersal pattern—which were held in a lower set of arms, thick pincers clacking above them—were trying to breech the walls.

A dozen figures who Nomed knew were putting up a defense. Mogits—who threw daggers while yelling "Magic missile!"—stood in front of a wispy-looking Manx who also launched daggers that resembled grey slivers of death. Tiffene summoned ice spears the length of her arm and, with a gesture, propelled them at the creatures, while Sam stood protectively in front of her, firing his twin long-barreled pistols. Golem—looking significantly different—punched at an invader trying to climb into the room from the desolate wasteland outside, while Durg did the same on the other side of the unfinished wall. Kitty fired her pulse cannon, and Fritz was an orange, fuzzy blur of teeth and claws. Croaker hunkered behind an ornate brass and glass bar, cobbling together some contraption or another. Elementius even helped, shooting small balls of fire that grew into massive flaming spheres as they crossed the space of the common room.

It was chaos, and it made Nomed smile as he joined the fray. He drew his bastard sword—wielding it with both hands—as his cape formed leathery wings and he flew at the attackers. The blade severed claws as he ducked under his compatriots' attacks, and he shot above the fracas to choose his next target.

Less than a minute later, Wanderly appeared beside Darome and let out a whoop of excited surprise. The small man whistled a long, sharp, piercing note and clouds formed in the dry sky outside, lightning jabbing down at the enemy force.

In a few minutes, the skirmish ended, and Nomed dropped to the floor and looked around. A score of the odd enemies were scattered around the wall that began building itself again, and the people within looked around with desperate expressions.

"So, that happened," Wanderly chimed.

"Indeed, it did," added Tilbert, peeking from around a corner, still typing on his hovering steno-contraption.

"What was that?" Nomed asked.

"One of many is what it was," Croaker grumped, rising from behind the counter with a small, odd looking hand cannon. "It's the fifth, no, sixth attack we've fended off. They're coming quicker and more often. Portals keep opening and dumping a bunch of weird things to attack us. We've seen gorilla-like creatures with brain helmets, dog-like men with lasers, snake-beings with spears and psionic powers that stunned half of us, and a few other things. The more the Traveller's Inn changes, the quicker the attacks come."

"Something is trying to stop whatever the Inn is doing,"

Tiffene murmured.

"Where have you two been?" Manx hissed. "Do you have any idea where Jack is or what he's been doing all this for?"

"He's breaking realities," Wanderly chirped. "At least that's what I think he's doing. He was just reacting to someone putting him in situations, but now he seems pissed and he's going on the offensive."

"But where is he now?" Mogits asked, unusually serious. "Why are we here defending his inn?"

"To answer the second question first," Nomed said, cleaning ichor off his sword as the creatures turned to a yellow mist and faded into the perma-daylight outside, "I think this is why he brought each of us here, at least in part. Let me explain before you ask anything else. I'm good at planning and creating chaos for enemies. I came to the Traveller's Inn a while ago, and only Wanderly and Croaker have been here longer than me. But I've spent decades sowing seeds to overthrow tyrants and stagnant rulers who crave the status quo. All the time I've been here, Jack almost never sent me away on missions. Same for Croaker and Wanderly. So, I must assume he has a different plan in mind for us."

"The endgame," Croaker muttered, rubbing at his nose. "He gave us constant information about everything and everyone's missions but kept us close. If he had a purpose for us, this might be it. Or part of it, at least."

"Exactly," Nomed began, then stopped as he studied the other inhabitants of the inn. "You've been at one another, haven't you? And where's Cogsley?"

"That bastard ate him!" Darome squeaked, pointing at Golem.

"Golem ate him?" Wanderly asked.

"Ooh," Sam oohed, "didn't really eat him. It was more like he forcibly upgraded himself when Cogsley fell apart. Not literally, but he was the sickest robot-thing I've ever seen."

"Seen a lot of robots?" Kitty snarked, causing the moustachioed man to redden. "Though he isn't wrong. It was more like Victavalen—which is what Golem is called now—absorbed Cogsley. They combined into one thing, or being, or whatever."

"I'm the guardian of the tower now," Victavalen said, his deep voice echoing from all around the room. "And the Traveller's Inn is not what it was. It's no longer a place for wandering adventurers and vagabonds. It has a greater purpose as the tower of time and bastion of…"

"Well, he did gain Cogsley's gift for talking a lot, didn't he?" Wanderly said, a bitter note entering his voice.

"What do we do now?" Mogits asked as the last brick closed the opening in the wall, leaving two thin arrow slits.

"We wait for Jack," Croaker said. "He owns this place, and I'm the pro-temp proprietor until he returns."

"That's up for debate." Elementius exchanged a pointed look with Tilbert before turning his gaze to Tiffene and the others.

"No," Wanderly said, pulling himself up to his full height and moving to stand next to Croaker, joined by Darome, Nomed, and Durg. "I don't think it is."

"Agreed," echoed Nomed, still holding his sword as he leveled a look at the remaining people who lined up on the other side of the room. "Fuck it, this is bullshit, folks. We're all being played. And maybe some of you are too blind to see it, and maybe some of you are all for it because it suits your goals, but I'm not for it. I hate being played."

"You know, Nomed," Wanderly chimed in, "it could be a double play."

"What's that even mean?" Croaker grumbled. "Are you talking about baseball?"

"I think he's talking about a double cross or a double agent," offered Darome.

"Ah," Croaker drew the word out and eyed the line of people across the room, "those I know about, quite intimately."

Nomed studied the old man leaning on the thick oaken bar, noting that Croaker had poured himself a thick, short glass of amber liquid and was running a finger along the rim. Croaker no longer seemed worried that his side of the room was outnumbered. For a moment, Nomed was flattered, but concerned, that the old man thought Wanderly and his own arrival evened the odds. Nomed was not confident about that. They faced a charlatan wizard who seemed to have found power from somewhere, a top-notch thief with depression issues, a temper-challenged quick-draw artist, a winter-witch, a professor of knowledge and elements, and a scribe. Okay, that last one wasn't so concerning, but considering the newly named Victavalen was standing on that side of the room and appeared to be intricately tied to the newly transformed tower, the odds were not in Team Croaker's favor in Nomed's humble, but experienced, opinion.

Beside the old man, Nomed himself, and his diminutive friend Wanderly, only a dumb-as-a-stump, philosophy-laden, half-ogre, and a knee-high gnomish illusionist with confidence issues stood on this side of the room. Nomed had every confidence in his ability to survive—even thrive—in difficult situations, but that didn't always mean those around him would do the same. In fact, it usually meant that the people closest to him physically or socially took the fall.

"It doesn't matter what you know." Elementius's raised voice drew Nomed's attention. "I am now in charge. This is no longer an inn; it is a tower. That means the management has changed."

"No, it doesn't." Croaker smiled, lifted his drink to his lips to sip, then said, "I've read the manual."

"He may be onto something," Wanderly said, shaking his head. "As soon as it wasn't a submarine, I lost all ability to control it and all management duties switched to Jack."

"And Cogsley shouldered a lot of those when he showed up," Croaker pointed at Victavalen, one finger extended from the glass he held, "and later I was given partial control, and Wanderly found the basement. That sounds like he had some ability regarding this place. It doesn't seem like it changing form changes what's on the inside, just the appearance and how it does things."

"Is a coven thirteen plus a leader," Wanderly asked, "or does the thirteen include a leader?"

"Traditionally," Elementius spoke before anyone else, "a

coven is twelve persons and one more to become the head, or focus, of the group."

"Like a baker's dozen," Durg's basso rumble tumbled out across the conversation, "I love the extra roll to eat. I love all the rolls."

"But…" Elementius continued, "I don't believe that is pertinent to this situation."

"It is according to Jack," Nomed said, stepping between the two lines facing one another. "He had mentioned the concept multiple times."

"Enough," Elementius barked. "I tire of these games and arguments of relevancy. None of it matters. I am in charge, and that is that."

The fat man turned to looked at those aligned to his side, eyeing Kitty with her arm cannon, Mogits the quasi-mage, Sam the quick shot, Fritz the vicious were-Pomeranian, Tilbert his scribe and sidekick, Tiffene the queen of ice magic, and Manx who was little more than a shadow at the edge of the room. Just beyond and in front of those was Victavalen. The automaton looked more than human. At more than two-meters tall, with shoulders a meter wide, and a physique that matched Manx's wiriness and Durg's musculature, he looked more than a match for any in the room.

"I think the odds are obvious," Elementius continued, "and though you may give a good fight, you would lose."

"Then," Croaker pulled out a pipe and lit it, "it's time to rally the troops. You see, Elementius, I've been around a while. I've been on both sides of the law and saw success. I've lived in three, no four, different times—or realities, if you prefer—and I've gone toe-to-toe with myths, legends, bounty hunters, masterminds, otherworldly powers, and so on, blah, blah, blah."

"All that means nothing," Elementius sneered. "I've outmaneuvered and outwitted you. You lose."

"No, you haven't," Croaker went on, puffing on his pipe, "because you overlooked a small detail. The devil is in the details, isn't that right, Nomed?"

"You're right, Croaker," Nomed agreed, having no idea

where this was all leading, "and I speak from vast experience with that idiom."

"Alright then," Elementius waved, a smug look on his face, "enlighten me on what I've missed."

"You brought in most of these folks," Croaker continued, his hand moving from his drink to his cobbled weapon on the bar. "Mogits and Manx were your recruits. Sam and Tiffene fell to you, as well. But you assume you have everyone on that side of the room. But look there…"

Croaker pointed with his pipe, and Elementius looked where he pointed. Kitty stood a step behind the line with her arm-cannon pointed at the professor. Fritz crouched beside her, his back to hers and his hackles up, growling at Manx.

"I've rallied my troops," Croaker went on, "people I personally recruited if you recall. You won't find it so easy to claim ownership of this time-travelling, reality-jumping, dimension-hopping establishment."

"Doesn't matter," Elementius said, a bit less sure of himself. "I still control the seed of the tower, Victavalen."

"No, sir, you don't," Croaker smiled, "does he Victavalen?"

"What?" Elementius furrowed his brow and gulped. "You can't control him."

"I answer to no man," Victavalen interrupted, "except the master of the tower, Transvartius."

"Oh," Tilbert said meekly, "and you don't control me."

"I certainly do!" Elementius screeched at the scribe.

"No," Tilbert cringed as he spoke, "I answered Jack's call before he brought you in. He charged me with taking notes for him. All the information I've gathered belongs to him."

"The tables have turned, Elementius," Croaker said in a low, gravel voice, "without any bloodshed. Unless you insist on some. But we will start with your blood."

"Seems there are three sides; five to seven to two," Nomed said.

The room fell silent, and Nomed felt a warm glow of affection and admiration for the older human. The demon-kin had seen centuries of manipulations and machinations, many engineered by himself, but rarely seen one so cleanly done as this.

Wanderly giggled and Darome joined in, both flexing empty hands in preparation of what came next. Durg flexed and cracked his knuckles with a wide-toothed grin.

"If we were playing cards," Croaker went on, "I'd say a bluff wouldn't work, and it's in your best interest to fold. Perhaps we can all agree to wait for Jack to return before we do anything else?"

Elementius slumped and dropped into a chair. Scowling, he tapped his fingers on the table and looked up through hooded eyes at the gathered group, each ready to fight.

"Transvartius," Victavalen said. "Transvartius is now master of this tower, and I agree to await his return. In the meantime, perhaps we can begin setting wards and defenses so nothing can threaten that return. When he arrives, he will settle the matter, once and for all."

"Drinks, anyone?" Nomed asked with a congenial smile.

## 10. Travellin' Man with a Plan

Jack smiled as the wasteland formed around him. Or rather, as he faded into existence above the unmoving form of a man laying curled in a fetal coil. The landscape around him looked post-apocalyptic, with blackened craters of glassed earth and thick beams of rusting metal thrusting from the dried and cracked ground at odd angles. Someone had hung bone dreamcatchers from a few and also from broken down turrets on long abandoned tanks.

Jack knew what caused this; it was humans being human. They discovered an alien race hiding on their world and refused to compromise. Instead, they decided on localized genocide. In other words, humans decided to kill every single troöd found rather than help them because humans felt small and scared. They'd have to get over their xenophobia if they wanted to join the larger community spanning the galaxy and beyond.

Troöds weren't a bad sort of alien neighbor to show up on your galactic doorstep. They usually didn't want anything but to look around and document things. They were naturally curious and helpful. But they were also instinctive geneticists and had changed themselves into a few varieties, including shapeshifters and a limited portal user who could open doorways to other realities, usually the ones that humans called demonic. But they wouldn't start doing that for thirty or forty thousand years in the future from this point.

The natural inclination of xenophobia in humans was funny, and it would be their downfall more than once. In this case, after the troöds decided humans couldn't be reasoned with; they detonated the tectonic fractures causing continental restructuring, released multiple human-removing viruses, and later a few series of bacteria that broke down metal and plastic, though most of that was more than a century in the future. After all that, humans triggered a humanoid biodiversity of their own species through genetic tampering on a scale they'd never imagined. Aeifain, Rokairn, and a dozen other species grew from the ruins along the with the surviving humans. It took tens of thousands of years after the collapse of society, almost equivalent to how long the human species had thrived as a civilization as reckoned by agriculture, math, and written language before it all happened.

Jack had travelled to the beginning of the end. Or perhaps it was better thought of as the end of the beginning. Knocked back to the bronze age and an almost ninety percent drop in population, the human species would soon be fighting nature; extinction versus adaptation.

This place and time (and the cyborg he currently stood above) were the first stop in a series of destinations. Jack needed to make sure he set events in motion that would complement his coming plans. He'd decided to start by jumping backwards. Once he'd covered this end of the spectrum, he'd pop forward and set a few more things into motion.

The man at his feet didn't look like a cyborg, because he was one of the first. He had nanotechnology implanted, a few genetic modifications, and a couple of weapons put into places that were once skin, bone, and muscles. The cybernetically enhanced man Jack stood over spasmed, causing Jack to look down.

"Byron Savage, I presume," Jack said.

"Jack?" the cyborg grunted, blinking as he tried to focus on Jack standing above him. "That you? Haven't seen you in what—a hundred, a hundred-fifty years?"

"Could be," Jack nodded and looked up at movement, a bare shimmer in the corner of his eye. It was a circling pack of mirror wolves. "Guess I should take care of them if I want you to survive."

Sighing, Jack studied the pack. Mirror wolves had evolved a camouflage ability through the use of gene splicing with chameleons. At the end of the twenty-first century, scientists were experimenting with all sorts of things, including that. They rarely got very far because they were missing a very important factor in their experiments. Necessity. Evolution demanded the need to change to survive and then to thrive. Labs didn't provide that. Nature did. Artificially placed genes went dormant but kicked in once many of these animals were no longer in captivity. But that took the collapse of civilization and lots of luck.

The creatures' short fur was thin, showing the hue-shifting skin underneath. The result was the ability to hide in flatlands with little more vegetation than scrub bushes. Between that and the instinct to hide in folds of the land allowed these wolves to once again become apex predators in a hostile environment.

Not wanting to kill such elegant beasts, and not wanting them to linger in the distance once he'd set the cyborg on track to the closest settlement, Jack summoned a portalling net. With a wave of a hand—the net following his motions at the distance of a dozen paces away—he scooped three of the creatures up. They disappeared, presumably appearing kilometers away in the northern reaches, and in the opposite direction of where he'd send Byron Savage.

Spinning, he caught one of the wolves leaping for him. Swinging his net in a wide circle, he caught another wolf darting towards his calf on a second side. The two attackers disappeared. He repeated this until he'd displaced most of the mirror wolves. The rest backed away to a respectful distance. Once he'd opened portals from a distant storm and blasted the broken terrain with a few bolts of lightning, they turned tail and ran, flicking in and out of sight as they did.

"Split the party," Jack grinned. "Guess they'll find one another, or become two packs. Maybe I should gather a party of people that I can play games with…"

Jack trailed off as he looked down at the man he came for. Byron's skin wasn't sunburned and blistered, but that was to be expected since the man had been infected with nanotechnology almost three hundred years ago, along with a dozen implants and bio-upgrades.

"Why are you here?" Byron asked again, breaking Jack from his reverie.

"I'm on a pilgrimage," Jack said with a shrug. "I need you to live again. Not exist, but live. You still have duties and obligations to fulfill. I'm going to send you somewhere you can begin doing that."

"Jack, I'm done," Byron murmured, his voice a ragged sheet of rasping breaths and rough hasping. "I came out here to die."

"Someone needs you, soldier," Jack said absently, knowing the words would trigger Byron's programming, both biological and installed wetware. "You're still needed to do important things. If you don't, then the world will die. If you do, then the world will be given another chance."

"But Jack," Byron's words were cut off as a segment of sky tore in a vertical line and a ragged rumble of thunder rolled across the land. A clawed hand the size of a Humvee, followed by a reverberating roar, came through the rift.

"So, they followed me," Jack said, his lips drawn in a tight line. "Time, literally, to get this show on the road."

Jack waved a hand, and the man fell through the crusted earth and disappeared. Jack knew Byron Savage would be okay. He'd sent the cyborg to a small town called Laundry, and it'd be the first step in the man's redemption. Jack looked towards the five-story tall monstrosity struggling to be birthed into this world and mentally prepared for his next port of call.

Looking down to focus his attention on something other than the monster best described as a kaiju, he noticed something on the ground. Kicking at the dirt, he uncovered most of the item. It was a dusty metal pole about as long as he was tall and as thick as his wrist, but not tarnished.

"Looks like someone left an artifact behind," Jack said, bending and picking up a silvery metal staff. Inspecting it, he spoke aloud again. "In good condition, eternal battery, light function, and probably a few other things."

He bent and recovered it and changed his own reality enough that the relic was attuned to his genetic code. The top of the staff lit up, and Jack smiled.

"On to the next stop," he said and disappeared as the horror fully appeared near where he'd stood moments ago.

Reappearing in a side alley of a busy city in the late twenty-first century, he took a few minutes to let his eyes adjust. It was night and a light rain was falling. Neon reflections of dozens of signs and ads shimmered in murky puddles.

"Atlanta, Georgia." Jack smiled. "Time to pass a torch to a torch."

It was an hour before Jack found the karaoke pub where the person he sought was performing. She was a woman in her twenties, still wearing her work clothes, though the lab coat wasn't to be seen. Her hair was still in the severe bun she wore at the chemical research lab, and the lights bleached her burnished skin. She sang well, though.

"Sorry about this, Savannah, but it looks like you'll be changing careers from science to magic," Jack murmured, sliding a leather-covered book with a note to the person behind the bar. "Give that to the songbird, would you?"

When the man looked up, Jack was gone.

Jack reappeared a few blocks away, outside of an antiquities and oddities shop that claimed to be mystical artifacts, which in fact, it was. But he felt the pull of two items in particular.

Stepping inside, he went directly to a glass case and pointed at two items sitting beside one another. They sat on dusty black velvet, a cheap table runner of white that had turned ecru under them.

"I'll take the onyx mortar and pestle and the brass singing bowl, please," he said to the bored grey-haired woman behind the counter across the room, "and also look out for a young woman named Savannah. She should arrive shortly."

He paid with local currency—regional and temporally—by stuffing his hand in his pocket and opening a small portal to a source of credits. He dropped a pile on the counter, scooped up his purchase and left without another word.

Outside, he looked at the items, then opened another rift and drew out a leather satchel. Pulling the strap over his head, he opened another portal within it and set the items directly on a shelf in his study in the tower. He tied that connection so it wouldn't fade, smiling at his own cleverness of making his own bag of holding. After a moment, he lifted the metal staff and slid it into the mouth of the bag and left it leaning against the door of his study.

A disheveled woman with two kids in baggy fleece jumpers stared at him, and he smiled at them.

"How'd you do that?" the bedraggled woman asked. "Are you like a Time Lord or Mary Poppins?"

"You may want to get home, there's a storm coming," Jack said to the woman, looking up at the sky then down the alley he stood in the mouth of. "In fact, looks like they're already here. Really, I'd skedaddle, lady, before you and your kids get washed away."

The woman looked up into the rain, and Jack turned sideways and travelled to his next destination. The woman looked back to where he'd been a moment before, and seeing a dry spot on the sidewalk where the stranger had stood a moment before, shook herself, grabbed the children by their hands, and hurried away.

In the shadows of an alley beside the junk shop, deep purple tentacles wriggled from a drainage grate and flopped onto the sidewalk, seeking prey.

Jack appeared in an apartment with dirty clothes and dishes scattered chaotically around. The prone form a man lay on the couch, snoring gently. Jack wandered around, picking up trinkets and odds and ends, inspecting them. He knew the young man on the couch—who would one day become Byron Savage—was drunk and wouldn't be waking up anytime soon. The man had a different name now, but Jack knew that after a few very specific military missions, he'd lose that name, and all memories attached to it. Well, most of the memories. They'd be replaced with an AI and commands from a quasi-nefarious organization called the T.A.L.O.N. Agency.

A computer sat in the corner, its dim glowing screen showing an AOL email account with an open electronic mail. Jack leaned down and saw the offer from the Colonel that he'd expected to see. The corporal on the couch was being offered a position in an experimental program.

"Windows 97," Jack murmured with a laugh, "been a while since I used you."

Typing out a reply, he hit send and turned back to the sleeping marine.

"Sorry, jarhead," he whispered quietly, "but destiny awaits."

Jack had the ability to go where he was needed with portals and find the place that was a problem. But he'd rarely used it proactively, preferring to be reactive. Now, though, he'd decided to use it quite purposefully to set up his plan.

"It's long overdue for me to go on the offensive," he sighed, "and besides, I'm tired of being manipulated by others. It's time I took control."

Looking at the scattered trinkets across the desk, he picked up a triskelion carved of petrified wood and the scrimshaw triquetra beside it. He felt the influence of the other slacken, and his own focus sharpen. With each item he collected, it allowed him stronger connections to specific times and places, as well as a general strengthening of his ability to travel.

"These will do for anchors to this point in time," he said, sliding them into his satchel and placing them on a shelf in his study.

A rapid pounding on the door told him it was time to make his exit. The Colonel had already sent men for the young marine sleeping off a night of leave. Turning around, he travelled again. He pulled his new staff back to him and changed his clothes as he moved along the timeline he knew so well.

He reappeared in an ankle length, rough grey cloak, and clothes of the era of the Dark Ages. He was in a short squat tower that smelled of earth and the midden heap outside of the open square window.

A group of eight men and women looked up from a large round wood table, their faces drawn and surprised in the dancing flames of the hearth.

"Scribes, are you not?" he asked, his voice slipping into a commanding gravitas. "You gather the knowledge lost or yet undiscovered and write it in tomes which you hide?"

It took an hour of convincing—which included drawn knives and many threats which he countered with a summoned pile a gold and by lighting his staff—for them to accept a wizard's warning words that they should keep doing exactly what they've already done. But he insisted they keep it secret from any in a position of power or influence.

When he left—leaving them with the name of Transvartius—he'd claimed a silver wrought uroboros and an ornate brass and copper hourglass in trade for the knowledge and coin he'd given them. They would become the founders of the Chroniclers Conclave and carry the secrets forward until magic returned in a thousand and a half years. They'd track the movements of the mystical and supernatural creatures that currently roamed the world and be prepared to recruit any humans who had small magical abilities. Telepathy, precognition, telekinesis, and other such gifts.

The rain picked up and fell as alternating curtains and torrents. The sound of snapping oaks mixed with the thunder and Jack knew the enemy had arrived again, though the items he'd been collecting made his adversary take longer to find him.

Travelling sideways through that reality, he materialized in a grand foyer of what appeared to be a rundown manor house. He'd meant to appear deeper within it, but something had blocked him from entering further than the entry hall. He felt the ancient being in the shadows beside a roaring fireplace rise, appearing as a tall man in the room to his left.

"You should ask permission before entering my domicile, Jack Tucker," the figure cloaked in shadows said, his voice like warm velvet on Jack's skin.

Jack felt himself teeter, the voice embracing him and gently rocking his body as his mind began sinking in a warm pool of memories. Shaking himself and connecting to the energy of travelling, doubling his presence and clearing his mind. Jack shivered like he had been doused with a bucket of icy water.

"You know me," Jack said, and using the energies at his beck and call, took a step closer and moved through the unseen barrier of will and spirit that blocked him moments before. "I would know how, for I did not know you until this moment."

A deep, throaty laugh came from the murk and the figure stepped into the light.

"I know you, Jack," a handsome man of indeterminate age said, "and you will know me. We shall be comrades, companions, and competitors for centuries to come. Or that's what you told me on an earlier visit."

"I arrived late," Jack sighed.

"No, you arrived neither late nor early, but at the exact time you meant to," the man said, "but decided to visit me sooner since the first time you did this at this moment. I injured you severely. I did not fare well either, if that soothes your mind. We fought for over 200 years before you could finally come to terms with me. I do hope you come to my aid in the future, as you did before."

"I'm confused." Jack ran his hand through his hair, stepping closer to study the man.

Jack had come here seeking the living supernatural, but this man was talking about things to come and the past. The man was pale, tall, and slim. He wore finery that was in better shape than the manor in which they stood. His face held no lines of age, but it was not youthful either.

"Jack," the man said, bowing, "forgive me. I make slights at your expense. I am the Baron and have walked these lands for over three centuries. Before choosing to settle here, I roamed the lands of Greece, Egypt, and walked the Silk Road to China and beyond. I started my journey under the rule of Constantine and even had some small part in forming the fifty ecclesiastical books, in a scholarly manner. That was long before I began dabbling in politics and the machinations of countries. I have the gifts you require and am prepared to begin the society of immortality you will ask me to form."

Jack's head whirled. He stared at the Baron and said the only words that would form in his throat. "You're gentry?"

"No," the man smiled and looked down, "it is but a name, or a title, as you prefer. Just as you will use many names, I have as well."

"Can you explain what," Jack hesitated, licking his lips, "how you…"

"Please," Baron said as Jack trailed off, "come and sit in front of the fire. You have a long journey in front of you after you visit me. Your enemy won't find you here, as they did in your other waypoints in this quest. Oh, surprised? You've told me about it on your other visits. The metal man will face monsters taller than any building we have. The singing woman will be approached by threats supernatural and mundane. The others you have here in this place are already being observed by men loyal to me."

Jack stumbled into a seat at a polished table, sinking into the thick padding of a high-backed wooden chair that could have been a throne. An ornate sword and a golden ankh the size of his forearm was laid on black silk across the table.

"There's wine," Baron said, gestured at a chilled pewter carafe and matching stemmed goblets etched with dragons. "I will explain. I will find beings you seek and bring them together. An ancient pharaoh that lived after the ritual for his death. An ancient serpent that came from another world to become a man. And the others. I will create this Immortalus Society you require, and we shall watch over your Chroniclers Conclave without interfering, even as they watch us."

"But how do you know all this?" Jack asked, reaching for the wine with a trembling hand.

"You'll have to do better than this if you're to succeed in your endeavors, Jack," Baron said, picking up the carafe and pouring wine into a cup and sliding it to the traveller. "As I said, you've come here before. When I was grievously wounded, a couple of centuries in the future, you brought me back here to begin anew."

"What?" Jack sputtered into his cup. "That would create paradox."

"No, it will not," Baron smiled. "You explained it to me. Something about the splitting of realities, or the pruning of one so another may grow."

The two men spoke until dawn threatened to pierce the misty veil outside. They discussed many things and plans, including a list of preternatural beings Baron thought Jack should visit before returning to the future.

Jack left with the sword and ankh, sending both to his study before his next jump. Baron was correct about the next leg of the journey. Jack sidetracked another 3,500 years into the past as well as making dozen stops along the timeline as he made his way beyond his starting point and into the world when steam drove airships and the many races that were once men rediscovered technology.

Jack met with Silver, who was happy to see him after the adventures they'd shared a few years before. Jack hadn't had those adventures yet, but remained silent about that. Sending Silver through a portal to a decade before Jack had dropped the leather tome on the bar for Savanah, telling him to set up a business and watch for an artifact in China. Silver gave him a crystal from a light booth along with a Dharmachakra.

The next stop was a young man named Cite in the lands before the Talisman had arrived, telling him to seek the lost desert empire when the time comes. Jack took an ivory rod the length of his forearm and a glass needle three times longer than a finger as the anchors to that point.

Arriving back in his study in the tower, Jack looked across the artifacts on his shelves. He smiled, knowing that no one would ever again control his destiny. And now it was time to show the multiverse that Jack Tucker had no master except himself.

## 11. The Final Countdown

Jack rolled the black leather blotter back to watch the events in the tavern below unfold in the crystal pane on his study's desk. He was no longer dressed in the bland beige outfit he once favored. A long, dark grey robe with silver piping and arcane accents on the cuffs, lapels, and shoulders rustled about him, his glowing staff in hand.

He looked at the shelves with his newly acquired items of power. Though they may not have had any special abilities when he took them, give any symbolically powerful items tens of thousands of years to steep and they now had many abilities imbued with the energy of the ages. People's beliefs infused them, and time had honed and extended the power within them.

Each of the artifacts now had purpose and focus. The sword granted him skill in combat. The staff focused and expanded his ability to manipulate arcane energies. The golden ankh gave the ability to heal grievous wounds. The light crystal helped him communicate across time and space. The Dharmachakra bestowed a connection to the Changing Wheel, the entity above gods who controlled fate, destiny, time, chaos, and more. The hourglass, brass singing bowl, ivory rod, glass needle, silver wrought uroboros. triskelion carved of petrified wood, the scrimshaw triquetra, onyx mortar and pestle, and a dozen other trinkets gave capabilities to allow him access to many other abilities. He was ready for anything.

"Things have progressed since I was last here," he murmured, looking back down at his desk and tapping absently on the surface of the translucent scrying surface, "and better than I had planned. I guess I must tend to the last handful of things needing done before I can move forward."

He knew who his enemy was now and was fully prepared and capable of handling him. He felt it in his bones and wouldn't let anyone or anything stand in the way of him saving the world. A couple more obstacles to overcome, then he could begin the next stages of his plan. He gathered a few of the relics, placing them about his body. He slid on rings and bracelets, drew a chain and medallion over his head to rest in the folds of the robe, and placed other items in waiting pockets and pouches.

Turning towards the door, he looked one more time at the shelves and sighed, wondering if he was doing the right thing. With a shake of his head, he dispelled his concerns and opened the door. He wouldn't let himself get in his way any longer.

Descending a wide, winding staircase circling the outer wall, Transvartius—once Jack—entered the room at the bottom of the tower. The chamber fell silent as everyone looked up at the stairs they hadn't previously seen.

"When it comes to life, everything up to this point has been a prologue," Transvartius addressed the group in the room, each staring at him with a mix of expressions, surprise or excitement, showing on most of the faces watching him. "Death comes for us all, but my life is out of sequence. Which means I may have died before my life was complete. I only have so much time, then I must end. And now I start anew. This is a moment such as that."

Nomed watched him, eyes narrowed as if trying to decipher the underlying meaning in the words. Hands twitching, the dichotomous demon-born maligned monstrosity struggled with his shifting emotions, and it showed on his face. Nomed was born to cause chaos, but had been raised to do the right thing. It caused a shitstorm of conflict within Nomed, but he usually went with what was most interesting to him. This time, that may not be the right thing to do, but he might go with it anyway.

Wanderly popped another cracker stacked with cheese into his mouth and chewed loudly, smacking his lips before washing it down with a goblet of what appeared to be wine. The small man, catching Transvartius's eye, smiled and pulled a small vial from a pocket and a penknife from up his sleeve. Wanderly then—with careful patience—cleaned his nails, catching any falling bits into the glass container.

"Great Lord," Elementius oozed, falling to his knees at Transvartius's feet. "I am ready to serve."

"Don't be a suck up, Elementius," Transvartius sneered disdainfully. "I saw what you tried to do to serve, and you suck at it. Self-serving is more like it. But it doesn't mean you won't serve *my* purposes, so don't get your hopes up."

The tower shook, dust sifting from above. Everyone looked around, and Sam rushed to one of the thin arrow slits.

"What in tarnation are those things?" Sam shouted. "They got tentacles and too many eyeballs, and they're trying to, yipes!"

Sam backpedaled as a thin, sinewy arm covered with mouth-like orifices thrust through the slit he'd been looking through a moment before. He drew a six-shooter and fired into the tentacle. It withdrew, the last length hanging by a rubbery thread.

"Those things," Transvartius said, "are reality trying to stop me from doing what I must. Even an ecosystem as large as one bubble in the multiverse has antibodies. And I need some of you to hold them off while I perform other tasks. Croaker, come forward. I have a very special mission for you and a few others here."

Another door opened, showing shadowy stairs lit with a flickering light that look like candlelight if the candles were dancing in a circle. The steps led down, and the silhouette of a man climbed up into the doorway, leaning heavily on the wall. Jack stumbled in, looking haggard and exhausted.

"So good of you to join us, Jack," Transvartius said, his lips in a tight line. "Your job is done though, and you may return to the basement, or I can destroy you. Those are your choices. I think we can do both now that I glance into the likely futures."

The gathered people moved.

Sam and Tiffene took a position at the arrow slit, firing bullets and ice spears at the creatures outside. Mogits positioned himself on the upper stairs, raining down magics upon the attackers. Manx disappeared into a shadow and reappearing at another to slice at invading tentacles, repeating the pattern once he'd removed the threat. Durg and Victavalen also joined the melee, grabbing and pulling the rubbery appendages until they withdrew or snapped.

Darome, standing on the bar, flicked an illusionary wall an arm span in front of the real one. Kitty slid backwards until her back was pressed against the actual wall, disappearing from everyone's sight except the illusionist's. Fritz was at her back with his hackles up and his tail stiff behind him. The were-Pomeranian nodded sharply towards Darome as the two slid towards the open basement door.

Croaker continued to lean against the bar. He looked across the items spread in front of him; a bottle and glass, a cumbersome tinkered together rifle of some sort, his pipe, and odds and ends of scraps.

"Croaker," Transvartius repeated, "come to me."

The older man hesitated, looking to Nomed.

"Don't worry about Nomed," Transvartius said. "I have other plans for him."

"We're not going anywhere until we know more about what's going on," Nomed said, his voice low and slow.

"Go where he sends you, Nomed," Jack said, nodding as he gripped the doorway to stay on his feet. "The reasons will become apparent in time."

"Listen to the specter," Transvartius nodded, "but I'll tell you what I can in the time we have. I need you at certain times and places to assist me. The time to leave this place is now, the time for your mission is now. I need to send you away.

Nomed. You and Croaker, Wanderly, Darome and Durg. This will loosen the final hold this monster has over this tower, and me."

"He's the monster?" Wanderly asked, pointing at the bedraggled man standing in the doorway.

With a wave of a Transvartius's hand, a portal appeared, showing a city of smokestacks with raised train tracks. People on the street beyond the magical doorway stared through the magical archway into the tower, gawking. Some wore tall hats and fine jackets with tails. Others held ornate walking sticks, dresses with bustles and carrying parasols, or drove motorized carriages with engines on the back, puffing steam.

"Nomed," Transvartius said, "I need you in this place to do what you do best. It's the only way to save the world from things to come."

"It's the future then?" Nomed asked.

"It's one of them," Jack said from the other side of the room as he flung a hand at the portal. The rift sparked and shrunk a bit.

"Quickly," Transvartius said, "it's the only way to break his hold and bring about the salvation of millions of lives."

Nomed looked at the crowd gathering on the other side of the portal and tilted his head at Jack, who nodded almost imperceptibly. A quirky smile appeared on his face, as if he saw something that changed his mind.

"Like any of that ever mattered to me," Nomed said, "but, fine, I'll do it."

With a flip of his leather cape, Nomed's clothes changed to match the crowd on the other side, and he stepped through. The portal snapped shut, and the building shuddered again.

"One less tie for you to this place," Transvartius said to the figure in front of the basement door. "Now for you Wanderly."

Another portal opened and Wanderly saw a series of island chains with gleaming towers and flying vehicles zipping under a shimmering dome of rainbow hues, dark storm clouds beyond and the shape of a dragon launching lightning at the protective shield.

"What do I do there?" Wanderly asked, his eyes darting to Jack for the briefest moment.

"Whistle up a storm," Jack muttered as he staggered into the room and away from the doorway and illusionary wall, falling to his knees.

"What you do best, my friend," Transvartius said over the other man, "charm them and then whatever comes naturally."

"It's all too easy," Wanderly popped another cheese and cracker stack into his mouth and chewed. When done, he looked up at Transvartius, pocketing the small vial he'd been fiddling with. "I do have a weakness for adventures though, and I *am* connected to this place, as well as the Highest Spire. I can find my way back if I want to. I'm good at finding ways to get places."

"I know you are," Transvartius said with a fond smile for the smaller man, "and I'm counting on it. But go now and break one more bond of this tower to someone who would grind it down."

Wanderly hopped down from his barstool, still holding his wine goblet. He walked to the magical opening. Turning back to the room, he raised the drinking vessel and fell backwards into the portal. It snapped shut behind him.

"Two down and a three more to go," Transvartius said to the man on his hands and knees in the middle of the room. "Once they're gone, you will no longer be able to control this place or me."

"I'll always be a part of this place," Jack wheezed.

"A stain would always be a part of this place, but it doesn't mean anything," Transvartius laughed. "Darome, you and your cohort are next. I'm sending you back to the rise of the magi, almost three thousand years ago. I need you two to get things started there. You'll be one of the most powerful spellslingers in the world as humans take knowledge from the aeifain and begin a new era of magical might."

"One path," Durg grunted, "leads to many places."

"Well said," Darome said, patting his big friend's forearm to be picked up. Looking down at the Jack on the floor, he winked at him. "I think we can work with this."

Durg raised the gnome to his shoulder as Darome settled his pointy cone of a hat on his balding head. The gnome spat on the floor, and Durg did the same.

"Send us through, O Mighty Transvartius," the gnomish illusionist intoned. "We have history to create."

The portal formed, ripping open with a gust of wet wind. On the other side, rain fell in sheets and a huddled group of men and women stood in a rough pavilion across from a contingent of a dozen lithe aeifain.

Jack reached for the door, his hand sliding through the portal, and a blue shimmer rippled across the surface.

"No you don't," Transvartius said, taking three quick steps forward and kicking the man's hand aside. "You won't be getting away this time. In you go, Darome and Durg."

The half-ogre bent and hunched to fit into the portal, stepping through into the rain. The magical doorway slid closed horizontally, then vertically, disappearing.

"Anchors," Transvartius said, standing over Jack. "I'm using your people to block you from going to the places and times where you might think you can work against me. It won't work this time, not anymore. Just one more, and I shall deal with you. Croaker?"

The noise of battle drew Transvartius's attention as a wall tumbled down and a score of small creatures swelled into the tower. Tiffene blasted the mass with a torrent of icy shards, knocking them back, and then sealed the breech with a plug of rough ice. The huge stones wobbled and rolled back to the broken section of wall, bouncing back into place and closing the opening as ice shattered.

While everyone's attention was on the wall, Kitty and Fritz passed through the fading illusionary wall and slipped down the stairs. Tilbert's keyboard clacked as he noted everything happening.

"Simple enough to roll back time in a small, localized area," Transvartius smiled, turning back to Jack.

"You've learned so much," Jack coughed, "and doing so much more than before. I'm proud of you."

"What you think, or feel, doesn't matter to me,"

Transvartius sneered.

"You're a part of me," Jack said, "and I'm a part of you. You can't change that or get rid of me."

"We'll see about that," Transvartius grinned and threw up an arm towards the bar.

Another portal opened between Jack and Croaker. A city of neon, glass, and steel could be seen on the other side of the mystical door. Cars zipped along the busy street, a span above the road. The bright signs of bordellos and gambling halls shimmered on their glassy surfaces.

"The Strip in New Vegas?" Croaker asked, then shrugged. "As good as anywhere else, I guess. Jack, take care of yourself. I'm not sure if this is the best way to do whatever it is you need to do, but I guess it may be the only way."

Shouldering his satchel, Croaker pocketed his now-empty pipe, picked up his glass in a toast and swallowed the last of the bourbon within. He swept the remaining scraps off the bar, and they flew the two meters to the open basement door, clattering down the stairs.

"I'll need money to get started," Croaker said as he tottered towards the opening, "but I guess that's taken care of."

"It is now," Transvartius said, waving a hand towards the old man's bag, which swelled visibly.

Jack nodded and smiled from the floor. "Go on, my friend. Things have a way of working out."

Croaker stepped through the rift, shouldering the cobbled together weapon as he did, and the portal closed. The building stopped shuddering, and the commotion of the attack slowed and fell silent.

"Victavalen," Transvartius said, waving a hand and the basement door slammed closed, "you're in charge until I return. I think this next part is best completed in another part of the tower."

## 12. Rifts & Rivers

With a wave of his arm, Transvartius transported Jack and himself to the study. The former stood behind the massive desk, and the latter lay on the floor, propped up on an elbow.

"You have a thing for grand gestures, don't you?" Jack asked. "Don't you think that's a bit melodramatic?"

"Showmanship is something you've always lacked," Transvartius said dismissively, "and sometimes these things are needed to impress the masses. You always preferred understatement, didn't you?"

"Understatement causes underestimation," Jack said with a shrug, then propped his head on his fist. "Did you bring me here to cow me? Impress me? Intimidate me?"

"I don't think that would work," Transvartius said. "After all, you've kept me running in circles as I tried to get ready for what's coming. I can't afford to have you undermining and distracting me anymore."

"You can't kill me," Jack chuckled, "because of that whole—oh, you know, you and me being the same person. I'll get under your skin one way or another."

"Every time you threw something at me," Transvartius said, sighing and shaking his head, "I blocked it. I have too many anchors now for you to even do that much now."

"What's yours is mine," Jack smiled.

"Jack," Transvartius said, "you brought your fate on yourself."

"Oh, I know," Jack went on grinning, "but fate, destiny, and karma are very real. And she can be a bitter and petty bitch."

"That's a bit sexist."

"Oh, he can be a garrulous asshole, too. They're not picky or gender specific. They are just as real as hope and happiness or depression and…"

"Stop it," Transvartius said sharply, "there's a war coming to Teurone from overseas. I need to get Torrents and the Kid to the same place as LT and that gnome gladiator. They need to be in place to deal with that. I'll need to activate the full portal network, not just on Teurone, but across the entire world for that to happen. I need to get that comet, Talisman, into the sky a half century before that happens. And then there's the matter of the second moon…"

"You have a lot on your plate," Jack said.

"Because you didn't have the spine to do it, Jack," Transvartius spat. "This is why you quit fighting, because you couldn't do what needs to be done."

"Oh, I wouldn't say that." Jack slowly pushed himself upright to a sitting position with a groan. "I've set everything up so it can be done. How do you think you got this far?"

"Are you taking credit for my deeds?" Transvartius looked genuinely taken aback. "Are you suggesting that everything I did was because you made it happen?

"Look around, Transvartius the Mad Mage," Jack spread his hands in front of him, "and tell me what you think. Why did you do all the things you did? Because I set you on that path."

"Fuck you," Transvartius spat.

"Fuck me?" Jack laughed. "Fuck you. It all comes out to the same thing. I made you, not the other way around. And I shall send you out to hunt like a dog. And you will obey, like a dog. Because that's all you are in the grand scheme, nothing more than something I'm using to point at a problem and send on a mission."

Transvartius reddened and swirled around the desk in a flutter of robes. He grabbed Jack by the hair, and with a grand gesture the ornate and decorated study was replaced by a cold, rock-strewn floor. A small stream meandered through the center of the chamber, a sparse set of wooden stairs leading up and away in a corner, miscellaneous pieces of metal scraps and gizmos scattered on the steps.

"Ah, the basement," Jack winced, holding the other man's hand that still gripped his hair, "where we dump the things we don't want to remember."

The spring burbled and tinkled in its shallow rut, moving from the font in one corner and disappearing into the wall on the opposite side.

"You know what that river is, don't you, Jack?" Transvartius thrust Jack's head towards the winding water, no more than an arm span across and half as deep.

"Time," Jack said, "at least how we see it in a physical form."

"And what happens if we drink from it, Jack?" Transvartius forced Jack's face closer. "What happens to us?"

"We're not sure," Jack slapped at the man's forearm, "maybe a fountain of youth, maybe it ages us with its passing."

"You don't know, Jack," Transvartius said between gritted teeth, "but I know. And I know you're going to drink deeply from it."

"Remember that stain we talked about earlier?" Jack asked as Transvartius dragged him the couple of steps to the water.

"What about it?" Transvartius asked, dropping to his knees and forcing Jack's head closer to the sparkling stream.

"It's still a part of whatever it's on." Jack didn't have a chance to say anything more as Transvartius thrust Jack's head into the stream.

Jack came up almost a half-minute later, sputtering and gasping. His hair was silver and had grown past his shoulders, his eyes sunken and dark. Jack's arms had thinned, and the skin on his face showed a deep network of islands formed of wrinkles.

"Wow," Jack groaned, "that works quick. But I have one

more thing to,"

Jack was cutoff again as Transvartius pushed his face into the current. Jack didn't struggle, but went limp. Still gripping Transvartius's forearm and wrist, the older version of the same man, the form folded into itself and shrunk into nothing but a skeleton. A beige stain formed on Transvartius's inner wrist, a brownish birthmark taking shape as the remains clattered to the rocky floor.

Transvartius stumbled backwards to look at his uncovered skin where Jack had held until the last moment. A shadowy tattoo appeared. A triple crow in the shape of triskelion with a single cloud above, a ring set in the center of the mist. Three bolts, one from each crow, encircled the cloud. Transvartius rubbed at it, trying to scrub the mark off.

"Doesn't matter," he said, rubbing at his temples. "He's gone, and I have work to do."

Turning in a flurry of robes, the Mad Mage disappeared. Two forms moved in the shadows of the stairs and Kitty and Fritz moved cautiously down the steps, the latter collecting the scattered pieces that Croaker had thrown down the stairs.

"Creepy shit," Kitty said, staring at the skeleton, "but if we had a bone to pick, now's the time."

"Yah," Fritz said, now in his human form, his bright orange speedo almost glowing in the dim light that came from nowhere, "and I see you made the cheap joke at my expense."

"I don't know what you mean," Kitty made a tight line of her lips, which may have been a smile or a grimace. "But what now? If we go upstairs, Transvartius's lackeys know we're not on their side, and they take that personally. If we stay down here, we'll die of starvation soon."

"I don't think so, Kitty-cat," Fritz said, using his pet name for her. "Time shouldn't work here like it does above. It's a river, and I tink many tings have been hidden here for when the time is right."

"That makes no sense," Kitty grumbled.

"Doesn't need to, yah?" Fritz grinned, "as is the way dat anything in dis place. We are where we need to be when the time comes."

"And when is that?"

"Now," Fritz said, still smiling, "or den. You got some stuff in your bag if you think we need to eat. Dip it in the dah water to make it make us younger, or stay alive longer, or whatever. I think dis is Jack's place now, and he's just waiting."

"Makes no sense," Kitty said.

"We wait," Fritz said, his tone serious, laying a hand on Kitty's arm, "and until later, we can always keep busy. Just you and me, like a honeymoon. And I still have the tings Croaker made."

Fritz squatted and gently placed the armful of things Croaker had left behind. Kitty looked, and they weren't just parts and pieces. They drew together, clicking into place, becoming three distinct devices.

"What are those?" Kitty asked, bending to look.

"A pocket watch," Fritz said, pointing at each in turn, "a zapper-gun-thing, and a really big compass thing with lots of dials and knobs. I am tinking dey are like time toys. But I don't tink I can use them, because dey look like dey hook to you there, and there, and there."

The short man pointed at Kitty's arm, neck, and hand, then looked up at his mate with a wolfish grin.

Travis I. Sivart

# Epilogue

Transvartius stood staring out the window of his study, rubbing his forearm. The distinctive markings had faded to the dullness of two-week old henna but were still there. It had been three months, relatively speaking. He'd moved the tower from the land of nowhere that it had crashed under previous management to a beautiful plain at the beginning of the Rise of Magi, an infamous era in the timeline he played within. Outside the leaded glass was the site that would one day be the home of the Nine Towers of Magic, each dedicated to a different aspect of the arcane powers.

The study had expanded, now three or four times larger than it had originally been. A circle in the center of the floor held a triangle of the artifacts he'd recovered. The staff formed on side, the ivory rod and the glass needle forming the other two sides. At each point was another relic; the golden ankh, the hourglass, and the Dharmachakra. He supposed he should name them something grand, because showmanship mattered. It distracted from the mundane ritual and time-consuming extrapolation of energies.

"Maybe," he mused, turning to look at them, "the Staff of Transvartius, the Celestial Wand of the Cosmos, and the Ivory Rod of Reality. The others could be the Sands of Shifting Time, the Golden Ankh of Life-giving, and the Wheel of

Change. Aw, not that it matters. Who else will ever see these things?"

He walked slowly around the circle that enclosed the ritual space, looking at the seven remaining items that formed the protective circle for the arcane ritual he was about to commit.

"Commit is a good word," he mumbled, "like it's a crime. Is it, though? These things are all bound to come to pass. I'm just trying to contain control and guide them."

The seven people downstairs were the outer ring, though not tied to the artifacts in that ring. And the others were the inner ring, also not directly tied to them. Was Nomed the sword? Wanderly the…what? He'd sent five away, and he'd make the thirteenth. But what of Kitty and Fritz? Where did they fit, and where had they gone?

"Maybe," looking at the silver uroboros, the legendary serpentine Mobius loop, the snake swallowing its tail, he smiled, "that one represents me, or I represent it."

He walked the perimeter, trying to mentally make sense of the things he was driven to do, wondering why he wasn't just enjoying the power and action. He was changing worlds on a whim, literally. Or was it something more?

"The Sword of Striking, Crystal of Chaos, Brass Bowl of Whistling, Bone Triquetra of Valor, Onyx Mortar and Pestle of Darkness, and the Crystal of Communication." He bestowed names on the other items, but still wondered which item of the dozens he collected, were tied to people he'd used, and were still being used. "Maybe the sword is Nomed, and the bowl would be Wanderly. Or is he the Dharmachakra? Would he ever think he's tied to the God making other gods?"

He stopped, his vision locked on a wall that was neither here nor there. This was all so familiar. Déjà vu, a term from a long, long-lost country, still applied here. He'd been here before, or at least remembered it as if he knew it would happen one day, but didn't have that recollection until moments before the moment happened.

"It doesn't matter," he shook himself, trying to shed the thoughts in his head that never help, and instead froze him to inaction, "I am here to call a comet from the heavens and lock it into orbit of this planet. That will give the…"

His mind wandered again. He knew what would happen. It would shatter the world. Magic would die and be reborn, bringing back the old, but mixed with something new, something that would allow the future to be changed from what it was.

Raising the hem of his robes, he stepped over the carefully drawn lines of gold, then platinum, graphene, and silver, and entered the center of the ritual circle. It might take thousands of years, but what he did here today in the past would change everything in the future. And a few things in the past.

Transvartius woke in a collapsed bundle in the center of the circle. He knew he'd called the Talisman to come. The portal he'd created would move it three degrees off course and in time it would join the circle this planet made around the sun. Then it would catch up, or the world would catch up to it, and it would orbit this world of Aetheria. He would break how magic worked when it collided with the single moon. The second moon made of this union would guide the future.

That would allow him to trigger the opening of the magical ways between places that had been lost or would be lost, eventually. They weren't even opened for the first time, this time. They'd existed when the beings from other dimensions came through, and that laid the groundwork for him to open them again once the invaders were repelled.

All the people he'd contacted would see to those things. That wasn't his job. While waiting, and before he needed to return from the point this all started, he needed a distraction.

"Didn't Jack used to play a game," he mused, "where people from one world acted as agents in another world? A world so different from theirs, they called simple laws of nature, magic? Why don't I go and get some of them, and let them be that? But in reality? Wouldn't that make them happy?"

He rose from the floor, dusting himself off and wondering

how long he'd been out. Had a thousand years passed, or only moments?

"Again," he said aloud, the shadows listening, "it doesn't matter."

Stepping over the broken and shattered magical circle, he flicked a hand at the thirteen artifacts and relics, and they flew to their respective places on the shelves and in dark corners.

He moved behind the desk and rolled back the black leather blotter. The crystal pane below flared to life, showing five people gathered around a table. They had stacks of books, papers, and piles of dice.

"Ah, yes," he smiled, a twinkle of madness in his eyes, "they will do nicely. A few preparations and they shall make a wonderful distraction until it is time for the next stage."

In the common room of a wonderful and arcane tavern on the ground level of the tower, seven people waited for the next bit of instruction. A mystical construction named Victavalen was in a close conversation with a scribe named Tilbert, who was jabbing a finger at a sheaf of papers.

The two knew they were tasked with creating an arena via a series of dungeons to challenge the boldest adventurer. They were only confused by one small thing; the adventurers wouldn't be from this world. They needed to make a place where others would arrive, stock it with monsters and mysteries, and use flying orbs of crystal to show it to the mighty mages of the great cities and civilizations for entertainment. It was the ultimate in arena games, allowing mages, wizards, and witches to watch the show from the comfort of their own lairs and abodes. They could even influence events for the right price.

In a corner booth sat an older, fat man who was brooding over a tankard of wine and glaring at the others in the room. He had schemes and plans, since his others had been destroyed. Cruelly cancelled and tossed to the winds. He swore his value and wouldn't be carelessly tossed aside.

He knew people, or at least knew how to reach people. He'd set it up so others would do his dirty work for him, and in the upcoming miasma of chaos, he'd gain the power he needed to overthrow Transvartius and his schemes, all the while never appearing to be involved.

A thief who once loved music brooded while his companion and once friend argued—almost with himself—how this next task would be an incredible opportunity. The mage who wouldn't stop talking about how this next endeavor would be the greatest of all.

He'd already planned a slippery one-two switch up of magic. Some guy would come in, all primed to be a powerful mage, but he'd have a rust eating monster devour the arcane artifact that was meant for the other guy.

The Ice Queen sat beside the quick shot and watched the others. The man with quivering red moustaches watched the woman, worried. He didn't want to be caught up in all this, but knew he wanted to be with her. Love had him all mixed up, but he knew he'd help her in whatever came. Even if she challenged the gods themselves.

The Mistress of Winter had other plans, though, plans that would allow her to break free of this place and the madman running the show. Ice could be insidious and cold, creeping in slowly so you never knew you were its victim until it was already too late.

Transvartius shifted the controls from his study above the others, smiling as he digested their schemes to take control of something they didn't even understand the scale and scope of all while plotting to use each and every one of them for his own schemes.

The Traveller's Inn had been reborn, and Transvartius had plans on top of plots to keep himself amused, all while saving the world. He'd just have to get his hands a little dirty while doing. Transvartius smiled as he scratched at the tattooed markings on his forearm of three crows and a ring on a cloud. He never noticed the bolts shimmering and shifting.

## Author's Note & Acknowledgements

Well, hello there. The creation of this book has been a long and wild ride. And none of that is important. What I'm saying is that this book is done, and I'd like to think I telegraphed many other adventures on the horizon. This part will thank many who helped, what went on in my life as I wrote this, and a few other random things, showing how life can kick you in the goodies and laugh as it moves on.

But we do have a choice! We can stay down, clutching our goods and crying, or we can get back up and move on, even if we're just limping. If you'd like to hear more about option two, read on. But—spoilers—it does have a few boo-hoo moments.

Here's the down-low, I was at a turning point in my life and my writing career. I had a few "Aha" moments and a few epiphanies (what a fun word, epiphanies, it's like a cloud of idea stuff) and I realized I'd been following a recently created standard for self-publishing authors. I also realized that it wasn't working for me. So, I planned to release a book every three weeks. This would allow me to complete all the current series I had in the works and set up new ones.

Then life happened. One of my cats died (I had ten), my son was in a head-on collision with a pickup truck while on his motorcycle, and my hard drive crashed, losing all eighteen plus books I had planned. Later in the year of 2024, other things happened that were worse, but we'll get to that (or not). Right now, we're going to focus on what (weirdly) affected my writing the most.

You see, I'm a pragmatic guy and I'm really good at compartmentalizing when I need to. So, the cat dying was rough, but it happens. I lost a friend, but he made me happy, and I lived with the latter part of the memory. My son's crash and injury, well, it broke two bones and had his GoPro running, so that would work itself out after a cast and some time. The hard drive crash, though, that nearly broke me as a writer.

Now, I know I'm not Stephen King or Brandon Sanderson (hi guys, call me!), but it still rocked my world. All my plans lay in ruins. I had a plan A, and a plan B. Plan A was to pay thousands of dollars to recover the drive. I don't have that kind of money, but I would scrape it together by lots of overtime and kind folks helping me. But that didn't work as the money didn't show up, and the company I turned to never even looked at the drive and kept changing its story. So, I had them send it back (it's right beside me, and I hope to recover it one day), and I turned to plan B.

Plan B was to rewrite everything I lost with only my memory to help. The hard part was I had a four-book series (five counting the omnibus) with a Kickstarter attached. Let me take a moment here to thank all the supporters on that Kickstarter for their kind patience. I was a wreck worrying about delivering on my promises. It was the worst part of all of this. Especially since most of them had supported at the level of the collection of all four books as an omnibus (that means all of them in one book, it's just a stupid word), and that meant rewriting three of the four books from the beginning.

I normally take about a month or two to write a complete novel. I do about 2,000 words a day or more. I do that most days. So, let's say I write 15,000 words a week. That 60,000 words in a month or more. I often do more. But this book took a lot longer. I can blame that on many things; 14-hour days four or five days a week for overtime at my day job, surgeries for my wife, hotspot internet via AT&T failing until we had none (finally have real internet via Starlink by January 2025), and a half dozen other things including mental and physical exhaustion. But I got it done, and here we are.

I'm excited about completing this book though, and that's a first in a long time. I have so many things in front of me I want to do, and I hint at many of them in this book. Silver & Smith has another three books (at least) and I have four other series in that world (five books each, minimum) to build that world. I want to continue my epic fantasy. I'd like to create a LitRPG (see the last few paragraphs of this book for more on that), and I have a few anthologies dedicated to world building that include characters from the Portals or Silver & Smith series.

Point is, I'm doing it my way now. I've done it the way everyone else said it should be done. I can only pander so much on social media. I have books to write, for goodness sake. I don't have six hours a day to spend responding to hashtags and groups, especially when it doesn't pan out. I'll write and work a day job in a warehouse or wherever pays enough to cover my bills, and I will write as a hobby because I love it.

They say to know your audience. Well, I don't know my audience. I don't know how to figure out who you are. Instead, I will write with passion and let my audience know me. Once they do, maybe they'll let me know who they are. If that happens, maybe I can find more and build our little secret society of clever ideas and kindness with just a little bit of an undertone of bitter sarcasm.

Due to privacy stuff, I can't post the names of everyone who supported the Kickstarter, but I want them to know I adore them and appreciate all they've done. I don't think I'll do another Kickstarter, though. Instead, I'll use my Patreon (https://www.patreon.com/travisisivart) or my personal Ko-fi (https://ko-fi.com/travisisivart) to offer behind-the-scenes tidbits. And of course, there's always subscribing to my newsletter (https://travisisivart.substack.com) and other such things.

This wraps things up. Thank you for reading this, and I hope you enjoyed it. I rise from the ashes of life's machinations and move forward with naïve enthusiasm. I always do, because that's how I'm wired. I have good friends, a loving wife, and a double-handful of cats to see me through the difficult times. But more importantly, they are all there for me in the good times. And I love them for it.

Read on brave and creative readers, and drop me a line at travisisivart@gmail.com to let me know what you think, or just sign up for the newsletter and enjoy this crazy ride I call my life.

Travis I. Sivart
January 15th, 2025

## About the Author

Travis I. Sivart is a prolific author of Fantasy, Science Fiction, Social DIY, and more. He's created The Traverse Reality, a shared universe that connects his cyberpunk, fantasy, and steampunk worlds, and writes characters who are as real as his readers.

Writing and telling stories since he was a young child, perhaps it was inevitable that Travis would call grappling with words and language a career—and loving every moment. He's privileged to share his work with a large and welcoming audience. Get in touch to discover more about his work, writing process, and future endeavors.

You can sometimes find him live streaming the writing and editing of his latest project from his home in Central Virginia, surrounded by too many cats.